Banking Affairs

Banking Affairs

SM PATIBANDA

PARTRIDGE
A Penguin Company

Partridge books may be ordered through booksellers or by contacting:

Partridge India
Penguin Books India Pvt.Ltd
11, Community Centre, Panchsheel Park, New Delhi 110017
India
www.partridgepublishing.com
Phone: 000.800.10062.62

"The outsider may mistake banking for a boring, staid, even sombre, business. But to the insider (one, that is, with a discerning eye and a twinkle in it) there is ne'er a dull day in the work-life.

It was more so in the ancient days (c.1970-1990), before men had yielded place to machines as money handlers and supervisors. Back then Indian bank offices were bright, breezy and buzzing outfits, somewhat overcrowded on the wrong side of their daunting counters with young, energetic and enterprising men and women.

The author worked in the largest of them for nearly thirty six years. Yes, 'from ten to five each day except on Saturdays where they used to wake him up and put him out at two!'. In this rib-tickling collection of nine short stories, he captures some authentic and hilarious vignettes of work life in Indian banks in those balmy days.

SM Patibanda (b.1944) lives a happy life of retirement in Hyderabad with his wife, children, grand children and a huge collection of assorted memories. His published writings include 'Lucky Sahasalu', a book of adventure stories for children, in Telugu."

CONTENTS

THE RIGHT FOOT FORWARD

Raju was staring at the question. He had no problem with the General Knowledge and the English sections of the question paper. He finished them in half the time of three hours allotted. His difficulty was with the section on General Mathematics.

In the eighth standard, he opted for Algebra so that he can continue to study Maths even after High School. The problems in the recruitment Test for clerks in THE BANK were of general nature such as Time and Work, Time and Distance etc.,. After struggling for some time he got the hang of the problems and finished the paper in time. After four months, he was called for the Interview. Another two months later, he was called for Medical Examination on 22nd of April.

About 25 candidates including half a dozen girls were selected for posting in the Hyderabad branch. The male candidates were sitting on a bench, waiting to be called. They were all asked to take off their shirts to save the delay at the Doctor's table. The candidate sitting next to Raju commented, "Here we are sitting bare chested with our shirts in our hands. I have seen in TV, in recruitment for the Army or the Police, the candidate's height, weight and the chest expansion on full breath were noted on the candidate's chest with chalk piece." Raju smiled.

As all the candidates were below twenty five years of age, the examination was perfunctory. The Doctor examined the chest and the back with the Stethoscope, asked the candidate to take deep breath. His ankle, knee and elbow were tapped with a rubber hammer. His throat was examined, his height and weight were noted and so on. The candidate was then asked to go in to a vestibule closed on three sides with green cloth. The open side was facing the doctor who was about twelve feet away. The candidate was to go in to the enclosure and drop his pants. The Doctor looked at the naked body and nodded that the examination was over.

The candidate was then instructed to report to Mr. Sarma, an official in the Establishment section. The doctor was hard pressed for time and was impatient.

Sudarsan, a candidate felt that the procedure was odd. When his turn came to go in to the enclosure, he asked, "Doctor, is this really necessary? What do you gain from looking . . . ?"

The doctor bellowed angrily, "Go in there and strip." Flustered, Sudarsan obeyed. After a few seconds, the doctor bellowed, "Come out."

Sudarsan obeyed silently and walked out naked. The doctor bellowed again, "Pull up your trousers." Red faced, Sudarsan pulled up his pants and joined the others in the Establishment section. Raju and Sudarsan were sitting across the desk from Sarma. Sarma was a simple man without any air of superiority and was quite friendly.

Raju asked Sudarsan, "I thought you were a shy person, but you came out naked brazenly."

"I was confused by the doctor's anger. I need this job badly. I didn't want to take a risk by antagonising him," replied Sudarsan.

Sarma overheard this conversation and said, "You have already passed through the recruitment process. The doctor can disqualify you only if you are physically unfit. Don't worry. Report for work tomorrow." Raju liked him instantly.

Sudarsan commented, "I really can't see any connection between my groin and banking."

Sarma replied, "The doctor knows his work. At least, that is what the Bank believes. Is your groin normal, like everybody else's?"

Sudarsan replied, "I don't know. I haven't seen the others."

"Nor did I. As the doctor did not comment against it, we can assume that it is normal," said Sarma.

"You made a lot of fuss about it," said Raju.

"Jobs are scarce these days. I am willing to walk in the Bank street stark naked for this job," said Sudarsan.

"So would I," agreed Raju. Sudarsan said woefully, "I feel silly and stupid over this episode."

Sarma said," You will do a lot more stupid and silly things in future. When you look back after you retire, you will realize that you are the dumbest and stupidest person in the world."

"What gave you that impression? I don't behave like this normally," sulked Sudarsan.

"I am not talking about you in particular. It happens to everybody. I have been in the Bank for ten years. Given another opportunity, I will not commit the acts I have done since my childhood that I regret and feel stupid about now."

"I feel silly right now," said Sudarsan.

"Cultivate a positive outlook. That will make life easier even though you don't stop making mistakes you will regret later. Tomorrow we shall verify your credentials. If they are in order, you embark on a lucrative career. Congratulations."

"Thank you, sir," they said rising to leave.

Next morning they arrived early and waited for the Bank to open for business, which was at 10.30 A.M. The main doors would be opened for the customers five minutes before the commencement of business. The receptionist would be in her seat by then and helps the customers find the right counter for their transactions and give them the blank forms required for their transaction.

They entered the Banking Hall through the staff entrance and seated themselves on the chairs meant for the customers in the corridor. At first glance she appeared to be beautiful. She was fair and short. Her hair was parted on the left side, falling short of her shoulders and covered her ears. Her smile was artificial. About four or five of us were sitting in the corridor while the rest of the new recruits were waiting under the trees outside.

The bank was located in the busy Bank Street in sprawling ten acres of land. The ambience was rich, professional and comfortable. Well-dressed men were moving about, getting ready for the day's work. There was a beautiful green lawn in the front, a huge banking hall, lot of leg room in the corridor for the customers and stinking Toilets. The banking hall is nearly eighty feet long, sixty feet wide, about forty feet high. The counters were running from end to end, leaving twelve feet corridor all around. There were chairs all along and writing stands for the customers. There were ceiling fans hanging from the roof and are about fifteen feet from the floor. The Hall was airy, cool and comfortable.

Sarma explained, "The Bank has an elaborate recruitment process. It is time consuming. When we need additional staff, we recruit staff temporarily. You will find a temporary employee working at the desk allotted to you. He will be retained at the desk. Work with him and learn your job."

3

After their credentials like the proof of age, educational qualifications etc., were verified, they were escorted to their places of work. The man working at Raju's desk looked sadly at Raju and broke in to a smile.

The supervisor at the place asked, "Do you know each other?"

"Yes sir. We know each other. We met in Madras," replied Raju.

The temporary employee said, "Raju, I am glad that I am handing over to you. I did not pass the recruitment test. I passed the examination for another Bank"

That section had four clerks and a head clerk. There was an Officer too, but he supervises a few more sections. Raju's section handles the accounts of a subsidiary Bank. All the transactions routed by the subsidiary Bank's branches through the Bank's branches are consolidated on a daily basis and the total amounts are credited and debited to their account with this branch. The activity was fragmentalised. Raju's predecessor had beautiful hand writing and his totals were always correct, which could not be said of Raju. Though his hand writing was not bad, his totals were always wrong. The Head Clerk was frequently losing patience with Raju. When they were free, Raju and the temporary employee reminisced about their contacts in Chennai.

After four days, Raju was called to the Establishment section and was handed over a set of cyclostyled papers. The heading was 'Appointment Order'. Before he could thank him, another set of papers were handed to him. The heading was 'Termination Order'. Raju's face went pale. His disappointment was so thick and heavy, it could be touched.

"I am sorry that my work was not satisfactory. Please give me some more time. I will catch up. Four days is too short to assess my performance. Please give me another opportunity," begged Raju

Sarma laughed and said, "I just wanted to see your reaction. Don't worry. Your job is secure. We hired you temporarily to enable you, the new recruits, to get acquainted with the work. The temporary employees will be terminated on 30th April. You will be absorbed on permanent basis with effect from the first May. According to rules there should be four days' gap between the temporary employment and the permanent appointment. Enjoy the next four days' free time."

Raju was dumbfounded and stared at Sarma.

"Report here on 1st May. That is a very auspicious day. Report early. There is 'varjyam' (inauspicious time) from 10.10 A.M. to 11.30 A.M. If you can report at 10.00A.M., that will be fine. Otherwise, report after

11.30 A.M. I do not advise the second option because, you will be late for work on the very first day of your employment," advised Sarma.

"This man is very orthodox," felt Raju.

Meanwhile, the other recruits got word of this and were alarmed. Senior employees and the men from the staff union confirmed Sarma's explanation. Relieved, the group went to the Irani restaurant, chatted for some time over cups of tea before dispersing. On the 1st May, Raju arrived at the Bank at 9.50.A.M. and at exactly at 10.00 A.M. stepped over the threshold of the staff entrance with the right foot forward, praying to Vinayaka for trouble free career.

Raju smiled happily at this memory. That step had changed his life. He is now 65 years old. He retired at sixty and fondly remembers the colleagues; some of them are no more. That step had taken him in to a world of finance, thrill, tension, worry, adversity, disappointment, joy, pleasure and happiness. But, that is life. He enjoyed his work in the Bank and was never frustrated. He worked until the last day of his service and retired with regret on superannuation. He enjoyed his service in the Bank the exposure to the markets, people and places thoroughly. He remembered the old gramophone record of the South African miner's song, "I owe my life to the company stone," and felt the same emotion towards the Bank.

He was startled out of his meditation by loud howl in the house and in the T.V. A wicket had fallen in 20: 20 cricket march. The batsman was walking back to the pavilion with disappointment, occasionally looking back at the wickets. Though Raju played cricket for amateur Cricket Clubs he was not very keen about this game. He was watching cricket only after retirement. Cricket is very popular in India because of its complicated scoring pattern. Unlike Foot Ball. Basket Ball etc., Cricket score is expressed as so many runs for so many wickets in so many overs etc.,. All the fielding positions have names. There is scope for interesting statistics and the players' performance records and history. It is a fancy game.

Raju said to the domestic audience, "Cricket used to be played for six days including a day of rest after three days. It used to be played by 'the gentlemen of leisure' who do not exist now because of modern day economic compulsions. Now the game is highly commercial."

A neighbour's son who was watching the game commented, "Twenty 20 cricket is excellent game. There is action from ball one to the last ball of the match. Nobody can watch the game for five days."

"That is the reason why they introduced this limited overs match. This is just a fraction of a test match," said Raju.

The boy declared, "In that case, twenty twenty match should be called 'testicle' as a fraction of a part is particle."

Raju smiled, "you are right, but you cannot call a game 'testicle', which is indecent and conduct tournaments. There is another interesting derivative from the word 'testicle'. It is said that the ancient Romans used to hold their testicles when they were making a statement in the Court or the Senate, giving birth to the word, 'testify.'"

Raju' wife complained, "Is that the way to speak to children."

Raju stood up and said," I will read about the match in the newspapers tomorrow. It is time to go to bed. Is anybody interested in bed time story?"

No body volunteered to listen. "Not today thatha (grand pa). We want to watch cricket," said somebody on behalf of all of them. Everybody knows that thatha goes to sleep half way through the story. Nobody had heard a bed time story completely.

"O.K . . . Goodnight kids."

———— ·◈· ————

THE MISFIRE

Dosapati Raja Rao aka Raju arrived at the bank by 9:15 A.M. He was quite early. Men were cleaning the premises including furniture and counters. Security staff were dressed up in their uniform and were moving about. They wore neatly pressed clothes and shining shoes. Most of them were ex-service men and they did not lose their discipline of the Armed forces. The banking hall was empty except for the cleaners and the security staff.

Sarma was already at his desk. During banking hours, the officers spend most of the time discussing matters with the customers and authorizing transactions. They do not have time for correspondence and verification of the day's transactions. They attend to these matters after office hours. They sit late and deal with these matters undisturbed. Sarma preferred to work very early when he feels fresh in the morning. Raju greeted Sarma and sat across his desk. Sarma acknowledged the greeting. He was sorting out letters according to priority. Letters requiring immediate attention were sorted out.

Raju asked, "Am I disturbing you?"

"No. I am glad that there is some company."

A gun was fired in the cash department area. That area was empty. Contrary to the training and instructions, nobody rolled down from their chairs and was crawling for cover. Sarma and Raju were staring at the area of the gun shot with surprise and curiosity. They did not move from their place.

A sweeper came from that area assuring everybody that there was no need for alarm.

"The gun went off accidentally when the guard was cleaning it", he announced.

"He could have killed somebody or himself due to his negligence", Sarma commented.

Raju said, "What will happen now? It is too early for an attempted robbery. Even if it was not a robbery, somebody would have been hurt seriously".

"Nothing will happen. Security Department will handle this situation. One bullet has to be accounted for. All the guards are ex-servicemen. They know how to handle the gun. There will be a safety catch. He must have released it. The gun was loaded. He did not notice that. That is sheer negligence."

Raju said "Security Department should be informed".

Sarma rang up the security officer and informed him about the happenstance. "He is already been informed. There is nothing for us to do. During the last ten years of my service, I never heard a gunshot. I never heard a gunshot in my life."

Raju said; "Nor did I".

"It is a very rare. The security guards themselves might never have heard the gun shot during their service in the bank. They become complacent. Any attempt at robbery will be a surprise.

At gun point, the staff will obey the commands of the robbers"

"What about the resistance. There are boxers, karatekas and wrestlers in the staff."

"They are all of no use against the gun. If you hear the gun shot, the bullet has missed you. It travels faster than sound."

"Albert Einstein said that the person sitting on the bullet will feel that it has hit the target instantaneously. The guns with the Security Dept. are antiques; I thought they will not fire."

"The guns are periodically checked by the Armed Reserve Police and certified by them".

They were silent for some time. Sarma broke the silence and asked, "You are a ladies' man, aren't you. You have a way with women. You strike friendship with them instantly. Others are jealous".

Raju replied, "I like girls. I enjoy talking to them and their company. But I avoid affairs with them. I don't take them out, unless they suggest it. I don't meet them after office hours".

"Why so. That is an instinctual drive".

"Once bitten, twice shy. I almost went to prison on a couple of occasions because of the girls."

"Why don't you tell me that incident? That will help me out of the boredom."

"It should be confidential,"

"Mum's the word. I swear,"

"Two years ago, I had a beautiful girl as my neighbour. The neighbour was a decent family with traditional values. We became friends soon. The friendship has turned into infatuation. I cannot tell who seduced whom, because both of us were equally responsible. She invited me to her room at night. The house was detached and independent. There were two rooms on the first floor. She sleeps in one of them. At 11:00 P.M. I jumped over the compound wall and reached the first floor through a branch of a mango tree in their compound."

"Quite an adventure," commented Sarma.

"After entering her room, I took off my clothes. She was wearing a negligee. She was pleased with the adventure and was giggling. I sat on her bed and was about to commence, when she lost her nerve and started pushing me away. I applied pressure and she started screaming. I grabbed my clothes and escaped into the night and jumped over the wall into our compound."

"Go on, I am enjoying this".

"Her family rushed to her. I don't know what she told them, but they didn't attempt to pursue and catch any intruder. Half an hour later, the lights went off in her house and everybody went to sleep. Had I been caught, I could have been convicted for attempted rape and a few more offences like deliberate trespass with criminal intent, etc."

"True, illicit affairs are likely to get you into trouble. Take the bank for example. Thirty percent of staff are women. That will be about seventy of them. There are only three or four cases of illicit affairs. Rani is sleeping with Giri. Suseela and Parvathi are cheating their husbands."

"How do you know that?"

"They think that they are doing something great and confess to their close friends. Soon everybody knows. It is difficult to keep such things secret".

"For an orthodox man, you have a lot of juicy information. Such affairs are always risky. The jealous husband may leave the wife or resort to violence. Normally, everybody knows about the affairs, except the husband."

"What happened to that girl?"

"She was filled with guilt and regret. Next day, she was making signs of apology and tried to save our friendship. But, I lost interest"

"That was a lucky escapade. Let me tell you about a leading case in England. It is Rex vs. King. A Mr. King eloped with a girl and returned after five days. Her father sued him for abducting his minor daughter. During the trial the girl admitted that she lied to him about her age. The judge convicted him and sentenced him for seven years in Jail. The judge said that according to law, abducting a minor is a crime. It did not exempt the defendant who believed that she was nineteen years old."

"Have you studied Law?"

"Yes. But I did not practice law as an advocate. I got the job in the Bank and I gave up the practice happily as I did not get a single case for six months"

"The advocate who wears new robes is treated as inexperienced. Your robes should be old and worn out indicating that you are a senior lawyer. A job and regular pay is a boon"

"Yes"

"True".

"What is the second incident?"

"I will tell you later. I am not in a mood for another confession"

"You are lucky to be sitting here instead of serving hard labour. The case you confessed is quite interesting"

Padmini was in the bank for seven years. She was looking after the Term Deposits. She lived with a premonition and was worried that she might commit a mistake. One day, an elderly couple accompanied by a young man of about 25 years approached her desk. They produced a Term Deposit receipt for payment on maturity. It was for a small amount of Rs 5,000/-. With accrued interest, the maturity value was close to Rs 6,000/—She showed them the seats. The young man remained standing. She placed a token on the table and pushed it towards the couple. The boy took it and waited. The receipt was processed and sent to the Cash Department for payment. The young man went to the cash Department to collect payment. Seeing that the couple were still waiting after fifteen minutes, she told them to collect payment from the cash counter. They said that they were waiting for the Bank's messenger to return with the cash.

Padmini said," He is not an employee of the Bank. I thought he was with you".

Padmini went to the cash Department and learned that the cash was collected. She returned and said "The transaction was complete and cash was paid. As far as the Bank is concerned the payment is made. The bank is not responsible for your negligence."

The elderly man contended "The negligence is yours. You did not ensure that the token was issued to the genuine payee."

"If you have any complaint, you can talk to the officer in charge or the Branch Manager."

"There is no point in complaining to anybody in the branch. They have to live with you and will support you."

The elderly lady complained, "At our age, getting simple things done like buying groceries and medicines etc. is a difficult task. We cannot go from pillar to post for justice. The options before us are complaining to your regional office or go to the Court. We do not expect the matter to be settled in our favour even after a long time. We will have to accept the loss." She was angry and frustrated.

Padmini was filled with remorse. She said, "Please wait for some time. I will see what can be done in the matter."

She approached Raju and asked, "Raju, can you spare Rs. 2000/-. I will return it in a few days."

"I have been in the bank for only one year. I did not save any money. I am a spend thrift. Why do you need so much money?"

She narrated the episode and explained, "I am terribly sorry about this incident. The amount may be small today, but it must have been valuable when they deposited it. They have no other income as they are retired. They cannot afford to lose the money at their age."

"Give me about fifteen minutes. I will see what I can do. Sarma is likely to have the money."

"Don't tell him this"

"I won't. But the information and gossip reach him inevitably. Nothing escapes his notice"

Raju went to Sarma asked for a loan of Rs.2000/-, "I will return it in two weeks," he said.

"I don't think you need the money. It must be for somebody else. Knowing you, I assume that it is for a woman. Am I right?"

"I will tell you in the evening. It should be extremely confidential".

"If it is a big secret, it will come to me within an hour. Here is the money," said Sarma.

Padmini paid the maturity value to the couple and apologized.

In the evening, Sarma said, "She did the right thing. It was her negligence, no doubt. There would have been an enquiry and the Bank will take action even if there is no complaint. Let us keep this confidential."

"She thanked me profusely for the help."

"There are people in the Bank who are afraid of handling the transactions. They live in perpetual fear of committing a mistake. They pray before each transaction."

"They must be leading a miserable life because of the trepidation. Nobody is immune from committing mistakes. It happens despite precautions taken. One could be a victim of a fraud perpetrated. Worrying can only aggravate fear and misery. One has to do his duty with integrity and sincerity and hope for the best," commented Raju.

"Well said".

THE HICCUP

It was 11:30 AM. The activity in the bank had picked up momentum and was in full swing. Suddenly there was commotion and shouts from counter no.16 in the cash Department. Somebody pressed the alarm. The security guard at the main entrance closed the doors. Other guards manning the staff entrance and the other gate at the back followed suit.

A customer, whose turn had come in the queue, was waiting for the cashier to look up after he finished recording the previous transaction. The customer pushed his cash through the hole in the vertical glass pane. His attention was diverted when somebody pointed two pieces of hundred rupee notes at his feet. He bent down to pick them up, when the cash on the glass pane was picked up by a person who disappeared with the cash. The commotion and alarm had prompted the security guards to close the entrance. The thief escaped and the pursuers were locked in. The security officer called the police.

The police questioned the cashier first and had taken his statement. He was not aware of the cash on the glass pane as he was recording the previous transaction in his scroll. He did not see the cash. The customer had only a fleeting glance at the culprit and could not describe him. He stated that he would not be able to recognize him.

The police officer commented that, "This is a difficult case. Nobody had a good look at the thief. We have very little information to follow up. There is only a confirmation of cash lost and that a crime was committed."

The customer claimed that "The cash was on the inside of the glass partition. The cash was lost from the Bank's premises. As far as I am concerned the money should be credited to my account."

The Chief Manager of the Bank rejected the claim and said that "Unless the cashier had taken the cash, counted it and confirmed amount, it cannot be claimed that the Bank had taken possession. The police also agreed with the Chief Manager. The customer did not press his claim. The Inspector of Police said, "Even if someone had seen the culprit and caught him, it is difficult to find the cash in his possession as the cash would have been passed on to an accomplice within seconds. If he is a known criminal, we may press changes only if we apprehend the majority of the gang. It is difficult to prove the case."

"So what do we do now", asked the Chief Manager.

"Nothing. I will file an FIR against the unknown person. We will also try to get some information through our network of informers. There is little hope of recovering the money. It is as good as lost."

The customer too agreed with official's comment and said, "We can only confirm that money was lost and a crime was committed. Beyond that, we cannot help the police in any way. I have no hope of seeing that money again."

The matter was therefore closed and the police left.

The Banking operations continued normally a couple of minutes after the alarm. The discussions with the police etc. were held in the Chief Manager's chamber. Counter no.16 was closed as the cashier was with the police in the Chief Manager's cabin and resumed activity after the police left.

The customer apologized to the cashier and said, "I am sorry about my claim, I have no intention of blaming you for the loss. It was stupid of me to divert attention even though such cases are reported frequently in the News Papers. I could not leave the matter without an effort to salvage my loss."

The cashier replied, "We have known each other for several years. The interaction between us has always been cordial. How much did you lose"?

"It was over Rs One Hundred thousand (one lac/lakh)".

"You did not resist the statement given in writing to the police. I am sorry about your loss. That is a large amount."

Raju was as usual sitting across Sarma's table at 5:40 PM. Sudarsan was also sitting next to Raju. Sarma said, "These things happen occasionally. Staff do not abandon their work to follow such situation. That could be another distraction".

Chakri joined them. They were chatting and commenting about the day's incident. After some more conversation, Chakri announced, "I found my soul mate. She is perfect."

Sarma said, "Perfect soul mates don't exist. You marry her and after few years, there will be some adjustment or compromise required to avoid

14

friction. They do not break up normally, but there will be disappointments. You are victim of the cupid's arrow, Congratulations. I hope it is not Leela. 75% of staff love her. There were at least 100 proposals for her hand. She declined all of them."

"I am talking about Ratna. Our families were neighbours for six years when my father was working in Bangalore and later at Madras. We were separated when my father was transferred to Calcutta."

"I noticed that you were paying a lot of attention to her, why don't you take her out."

"She doesn't accept my invitations. She had come to a restaurant a couple of times."

"May be she does not want to commit herself without some positive signal from you. A couple of lunches do not indicate anything as you have known her since childhood."

"What did you talk about during the lunches" intervened Raju.

"Only childhood memories and what we did during the period between our separation at Madras and reunion in the Bank."

"Ratna is quite good looking and well behaved. There is no comparison to Leela", said Sudarsan.

"Leela's sister appears to be more mature and intelligent" said Chakri.

"That is not her sister. She is her mother", said Sarma.

"Wonderful. If she takes after her mother, Leela would be beautiful even in old age".

"Her father is quite handsome too", said Sarma.

"Are your families in touch during all these years", asked Raju.

"I don't know, I did not see them after the separation," replied Chakri

"Do you rate her as interested"?

"I cannot say. She was quite friendly and appeared to be accepting me as a childhood friend".

"Do you anticipate any hurdles?"

"Yes, our castes are different. My family is vegetarian by tradition, while her family is non-vegetarian. My parents are very particular about compatible horoscopes."

"Leela must be the soul mate of Raju. He spends a lot of time with her," said Sudarsan

Sarma laughed and said, "Raju was once bitten and twice shy. He wouldn't do anything drastic".

Raju said, "I do not know what Love is. I wonder if I can recognize it when Love strikes me. It is true that I spend a lot of time with the girls, but I got into trouble because of that weakness".

"What kind of trouble?" asked Chakri?

'I will tell you about an incident I faced. I cannot tell you the events that were night mares. When I was working in a private firm in Madras, I was approached by three girls, two of whom I knew. One of my friends explained that the third girl committed an indiscretion and fell in love with a college mate. She missed her periods and expected that she is pregnant. She comes from a rich and conservative family from North India.'

'Why are you telling me all this, I asked.'

'She needs an abortion.'

'She can approach her lover.'

'He said that the girl was too fast and easy and must have slept with others. He cannot marry a person with such character.'

'What do you want?'

"Please help her. She needs an abortion. Her family is very particular about their honour."

"I have taken her to a nurse in a private hospital and arranged for the abortion. We pooled our savings and spent it for the termination of pregnancy and post operation care". Sudarsan and Chakri laughed heartily at Raju for the termination of pregnancy caused by another man.

Sarma said "Raju, I admire you. You had the compassion for the girl. What happened to her"?

"Her parents learned of this and admonished her. They approached her lover's family with the marriage proposal. The boy's parents were happy with the proposal as the girl's parents were rich and influential and the boy too agreed to marry her. But the girl refused to marry him despite pressure from her parents. Six months later, she was married to a Software Engineer from U.S. When informed about her pregnancy, he said that he was not concerned with her past and was only looking forward to a happy marriage in future. He was obviously influenced by the western society. Resident Indians want virgins and do not accept sex before marriage".

After office hours, as usual, Raju was sitting at Sarma's desk. Sudarsan and Chakri joined him.

Sarma said "You guys got secure jobs. Your parents must be receiving marriage proposals".

"I don't believe in arranged marriages. There will be no love in the marriage. It will be like a job for both of them", declared Chakri.

16

"How do you explain the marriages that last until one of the couple dies? Love marriages fail often. Infatuation is usually mistaken for love," said Raju.

"You don't fall in love with the strangers. You have to meet your future life partner a number of times and understand her or his attitudes and expectations. In arranged marriages, the association for some time will make them love each other. The failure of arranged marriages is less compared to the love marriages" said Sudarsan.

Sarma commented, "That is because divorce is looked down up on by our society. It is difficult to find another partner for the divorcee. The partner may be financially independent, but becomes lonely. The security of marriage is lost."

"You commit one mistake and you will regret it for the rest of your life", said Raju.

"I am in love. I am quite sure that she is my soul mate", said Chakri.

"Did you express your love to her?"

"No I don't want to risk losing her company, by expressing my intention prematurely."

"That may be the problem. Naturally she would not like to commit herself to you, if it does not lead to some positive response from you. As you want to marry her, propose to her. If she says yes and marriage takes place, I lose a good employee," Sarma.

"Why? She may not be willing to give up her job."

"The bank has a rule that the husband and the wife cannot work in the same branch. In a large branch like this, one of you may be transferred to another department. I will not surrender you."

Raju said, "You have been talking to her for more than one year. The uncertainty should not continue any longer."

Chakri said, "I am not as skilful as you are".

"I am a psycho; I lose interest in the woman after getting to know of her weakness or domestic problems. I continue to maintain the same relationship but will not let it become serious. I disappoint them and make them angry occasionally, as I do not allow the relationship become serious".

"You strike friendship with girls almost instantly and sustain it for long".

"Raju is quite handsome and has communication skills. He possesses the charm and attracts people. His magnetic charm attracts everybody, but is largely noticed in the case of ladies. He is quite intelligent and confident in his approach to events in life," said Sarma.

"Thank you. I hope you are right. I understand the love between the parents and children and between blood relations like brother and sisters. The love between a male and female is difficult to distinguish from infatuation. The spouse may be disappointed if the partner does not live up to the expectations."

"You spent enough time with her. You can raise the matter of marriage with her. Has she given any hint as to her opinion on the subject", asked Sudarsan.

"No, my fear is that I may not be up to her expectations", replied Chakri.

"You better settle the matter without any more loss of time," advised Sudarsan.

"I told you about the two impediments to the parental consent. She could be reluctant to defy her family."

Raju intervened, "I have the same problem with my parents. I think that the parents will reconcile to the marriage after some time, if everything goes on smoothly between the two."

"She sits next to Suvasini. I will have to find her alone."

"Ignore Suvasini. Go ahead and talk to her. Suvasini could be a good witness".

Sarma said, "Let me check the Panchangam (Almanac). Tomorrow is an auspicious day. There is Varjyam, (inauspicious time) from 4:26 to 5:15. Don't propose during that period. As your intentions are honest, go ahead"

"Thank you for your advice. Tomorrow is the day."

The following day he approached Ratna at her desk around 12:15 PM and started talking.

"Our families were neighbours for a long time in our childhood. We were separated because of the transfers.

We met again after a long time in the bank. My parents are looking for suitable marriage alliance for me. It could be the same in your case too. You are not the same Ratna. I have known in my child hood. You grew up to be very pretty. I was impressed when I saw you in the Bank. Talking to you has always been a pleasure and I enjoy your company. I would have been happier if you had agreed to spend more time with me outside the Bank. You did not come out with me. I think, I love you and will be happy to spend my life with you. Our parents are looking for suitable life partners. I want to marry you. Will you . . . ."

He was interrupted by a long and loud fart from Suvasini. He was taken aback. Suvasini looked up and grinned at him stupidly, with embarrassment. Ratna looked up and grinned. Crest fallen, Chakri mumbled and left the place.

Sarma and Sudarsan observed the incident and realized that something went wrong. When Chakri narrated the incident in the evening, Sarma asked, "Why did you respond to Suvasini, you should have pursued the matter.

"I was taken aback, I mumbled. 'Bless you' and walked away".

"That is not proper; 'Bless you' is for sneeze"

"What do you say in the case of a fart?"

"Nothing, you hold your breath as long as possible".

"My worry is that a girl like Ratna would by now have a man. The parents might already have found a suitable boy for her. I do not expect her to be free.

Suvasini came to me and apologized. She has no idea about Ratna's feelings."

Suvasini apologized to Ratna and said, "I am sorry. I interrupted a very important conversation of your life. I got the urge when Chakri came to our desks. I put it on hold. But, he was beating about the bush. Naturally the harder you hold, the louder it comes. Next time he comes here, I will leave my desk for a few minutes."

"Don't worry about it. It is not in your hands. I mean, it is not in your control. What ever happened must be for our good only. You don't have to leave your desk. Please stay where you are," said Ratna.

"Aren't you going to accept him?"

"He did not propose and I did not have to answer"

"Oh, I am sorry"

Suvasini later approached Chakri and said, "Chakri, I am sorry about what happened. Please forgive me."

"Did she comment anything? Did she show her reaction to what I said?"

"Nothing. I do not know how she felt about you. It is the food at the working women's hostel that played the villain."

In the evening, Raju, Sudarsan and Chakri assembled at Sarma's desk. They listened to Chakri's narration. Sarma said, "Even though you did not ask her, Ratna must have got the message. Leave her alone for a few days.

Smile at Ratna whenever your eyes meet, but do not approach her. She may consider it as pestering. We do not want a complaint from her."

"Is it a good omen?" asked Chakri.

"How did the fart sound?"

"It was like the chain of crackers bursting in Deepavali"

"That is celebration. You will get the wife you want"

"Thank you," said Chakri and left.

Sudarsan said, "I do not know of any omens read from a fart".

Sarma replied, "Nor do I. I tried to lift his spirits. Imagine his heart break. The seriousness of the proposal was ruined by the fart."

A week later, Raju and Sudarsan were sitting at Sarma's table as usual when Chakri came beaming and distributed sweets to the three of them.

"I proposed to Ratna during lunch and she accepted. A few minutes back, Ratna's parents approached my family and proposed the alliance. My dad called me. I confirmed that I proposed to her and that she accepted. I am going to her house now to seek her parent's approval."

Next morning, Chakri requested Sarma for permission to leave early as his family was invited to visit Ratna's house".

"You may leave early at 3:30 P.M. Ratna must be in need of permission".

"No, she is taking today off and has applied for leave. I have to take a length of Jasmine buds knit together, roses, fruits and sweets as we are visiting the bride to be. Both the families will discuss the arrangements for the wedding. My parents have agreed to the marriage."

"This situation is very bad. It is difficult to accept it. I am losing a beautiful and efficient employee", said Sarma beaming with a radiant smile.

THE LAPTOP

Raju was at his desk at 5:00 P.M. preparing for the closure of day's work. Leela came to him and said, "Raju can I talk to you for a few minutes. The matter is quite serious".

"Go ahead"

"I am getting threatening calls. I am afraid".

"That is the price you pay for being a beauty".

"This is not a joke. The telephone operator says that the caller is asking for the extension number and is not asking for me by name. As I sit closest to the extension, I receive the calls and attend to them".

"What does he want?"

"He wants to marry me. I told him that he can approach me directly and propose. I assured him that I will not complain against him because people do propose to me and if I like him I may agree. If not I will say 'no'".

"He doesn't want to take a no for an answer. Is that so"?

"He did not say so in so many words. I explained to him that it is impossible to agree to a marriage without even seeing him".

"He must be a customer. Bank staff do not call you from outside and they know that they can approach the subject, as many people have done".

"I do not take offence if they want to marry me. I cannot stop people asking me to marry them. I can only decline the proposal. I take care not to offend them. I am not arrogant".

"Ask him for the personal details".

"He says he's rich, educated abroad, a sportsman and is twenty seven years of age. He says, he is tall and fair and is considered good looking".

"Appears to be eligible for marriage. Ask him to meet you".

"I did. Oh! There is a call for me. It may be the same man. Will you talk to him"?

"OK", said Raju.

It was the anonymous caller.

Leela made a sign and spoke into the phone, "Sir, this is not taking us anywhere. Please talk to my friend. He is known in the Bank as Raju. Raju, please talk to a fan of mine".

Raju received the phone and said, "Good Evening Sir. You appear to be well educated, well placed and good looking. You can approach her directly or talk to her parents. The way you are approaching will not get you anywhere. Be practical. If you persist in your efforts this way, you will definitely get a 'No' for an answer".

"Are you her friend?"

"Yes. A friend and colleague"

"Have you proposed to her? If she has passed on the phone to you, it means that you are a close friend", said the caller.

"I am her close friend. I have not asked her to marry me"

"Why not"

"She is not my league. I am a clerk in the Bank. She is too good and very much above my level".

"You appear to have clarity and wisdom in your approach to life. I cannot take a 'no' from her. If I do not get her, my life would be miserable and full of regret. I am very jealous."

"That is not correct. You are likely to commit a crime. You will end up in a prison and will have plenty of time to regret your action. If that is the way you think, we will call the Police".

"I know that, but I am helpless. I love her. I must have her. Will you help me"?

"Certainly. I cannot promise you the marriage with her and will not be involved in anything illegal".

"O.K. I will call you and inform you of the rendezvous. I want to get out of this crazy mess".

"Bye, Sir".

Raju hung up and told Leela, "Don't worry. The matter is going to be settled. He is hopelessly infatuated with you. He is going to be reasonable. Will you consider marrying him if the personal details are true"?

"I don't know. I am inclined to decline".

"Please give it a thought. He has agreed to meet me. I will ask Sarma to come with me. He asked me if I have proposed to you. I told him that we are very good friends".

"Now that the subject is raised, why didn't you ask me to marry you"?

"I am not your level. I cannot make you happy with my meagre earnings. After a few years you will be disappointed with me. Will you accept if I propose"?

"I take it as a proposal. I will think about it and give you my answer in two days".

"Forget it. I am not proposing to you. I am happy to be your friend. I do not intend to pollute our relationship".

"Now that you have taken control of the situation, I am relieved".

"He will be reasonable".

Raju returned to his work. At 5:30 P.M., he closed his desk and waited for Sarma, who was not in his seat.

Surayah, the sweeper was passing by and smiled at him.

"You are making advances to Leela, is it not? Wish you the best of luck, you will succeed. I can glean an intimate relationship developing".

"You are wrong. We are friends. I am not that kind of man. You seem to be imagining".

"Sure. Nobody is that kind until they get an opportunity".

"You have a dirty mind".

"What is the point in talking to them if you are not going for intimacy? Men and women are meant to have sex".

"I can't agree with you. I have been talking to you quite closely. Do we have sexual relationship"?

"My case is different. Perhaps you do not fancy me. I have no complaint". Surayah grinned and walked away.

Two days later Raju received phone call from the anonymous caller. "Mr. Raju, I spoke to you two days ago regarding Ms.Leela. Can you meet me this evening"?

"Yes. Where shall we meet"?

"Will Taj Banjara be convenient for you? You can be there at 7:00 P.M".

"How do we recognize each other"?

"I will be at the restaurant wearing a black blazer with a rose tucked at the first hole on the neck line on the right side. The left hand pocket will bear the logo of the Andhra Pradesh Boxing Association".

"O.K. Can I bring a colleague?"

"Please do. By discussing the matter we can resolve the problem. If I get it off my chest, I can think clearly".

Sarma and Raju were at the hotel restaurant at 7:00 P.M sharp. They found a man sitting at the table near the entrance wearing a blazer with a rose near the neck.

As they moved towards him, he got up and introduced himself.

"I am Ravi Shankar. I am glad you came. You are Mr. Raju, I presume".

"No, I am Sarma. This is Raju"

"Raju? You are quite young. Younger than me. You spoke wisely and are cautious. I realized that I am behaving stupidly".

"It happens to some people. You spoke to me that day. You did not insist on speaking to the lady only".

"Are you a Boxer", asked Sarma.

"I have been boxing since my school days. After graduation in Engineering, I did MBA at the Boston University. I continued boxing in Boston. I am not a champion or professional. I am an amateur. Because of my experience, I am recognized by the Boxing Association".

"Wow, you are an Engineer with a management degree from an American University and a sportsman too. What do you do for a living", asked Sarma.

"My father is an Industrialist. He has a chemical factory in Hyderabad, a sugar factory near Tirupathi, a factory near Bhimavaram that exports shrimp mainly to Japan".

"Are you the only son?"

"Yes. All the factories are said to be our own, but we have only the controlling interest in these companies. There are other shareholders, both individual and corporate. We are the sole owners of a holding company named Mukkapati & Son (P) Ltd. Our industries are held in the name of the holding company".

"You are endowed with good looks, education, and wealth and sporting interest. Why do you behave so badly", asked Raju.

"Thank you. I don't normally visit the banks. That area is taken care of by the Accounts Departments who have Chartered Accountants and a Finance Manager. I came to your bank with a friend who is your borrower. I saw that woman and fell in love with her at first sight. I was so deeply mesmerized by her that I was not thinking rationally. I did not share my feelings with anybody".

"That was a mistake. You would not have suffered the pangs of love and became drastic".

"Even though I was talking to her with desperation, I have no criminal intention".

"We can appreciate your predicament. But the telephone calls to her are out of character".

"Yes, that was stupid of me"

"No woman is worth a prison sentence, no man is worth the great sacrifice. There will always be some disappointment and discord in a marriage. They may not result in broken marriages, as the couple will adjust and adapt to the situation", said Sarma.

"If you want to talk to her, we will take you to her house now".

"That will not be necessary. My heart is clear now. I won't bother her again. I understand that I am a stranger and cannot expect her to marry me".

"I can assure you that your proposal will be declined on the spot without even discussing the matter".

"Yes. That is certain. I am sorry. I have been talking. What will you have before dinner? I am going to have a beer".

Sarma said, "I don't drink. Some fruit juice will be enough for me. As for dinner, if you insist, I will have something vegetarian".

Raju said, "I am also vegetarian. I will have some whisky and water. You know our phone numbers. Can we have your card"?

"That won't be necessary. I am not going to call her. I may not meet you again. I am surprised at my own indiscretion and behaviour. Now I feel relieved and happy. Thanks for coming and clearing my head".

After dinner, he bid farewell and left.

He never called Leela or Raju or Sarma again.

After she listened to the narration of the events, commented, "He is a gifted man. He is rich, educated, sportsman and very good looking. Even if all that is true, I cannot entertain his proposal as he is a total stranger. I will not take the risk".

"So many people have asked you to marry them. So far, you have not accepted any one. Do you have somebody in mind," asked Sarma.

"I will choose when the time comes. My mother cautions me almost every day. One mistake at this stage and I will regret for the rest of my life. People advise me to take up modeling or acting. I am considered beautiful in the bank. I am photogenic too. But in the field of modeling and acting, everybody is beautiful. Success does not come easily. It depends on the story, music, dance and lot of luck. My parents are also against this. They say that it is difficult to marry and settle down. The competition is heavy. Besides, I am not interested".

Thus the affair of unwanted calls was closed.

As Raju was leaving the premises, Surayah and Seetamma accosted him. He smiled pleasantly. Seetamma asked, "Raju Sir, Can you lend me ten rupees".

Raju obliged.

She said, "I may not return the money, but I will give you an advice that is worth thousand times more".

Raju smiled, "I know that you will not return the money"

Seetamma laughed and said, "Adultery is considered a sin. But everybody wants to commit it. It is a very pleasant sin. I will say that again for you. Everybody craves sex. There is nobody who is not anxious for illegitimate relationship. You are wasting your youth".

"You are missing the opportunities," said Surayah.

"What if the husband finds out and leaves her. I will be stuck with a woman I don't want to live with. The husband could be jealous and kill me".

"After a few years of marriage with children, the husband will put a stop to the affair and pretend that nothing happened. He would or might already have an affair with somebody".

Raju said, "Thank you" and walked away.

Next morning Raju woke up early. After the shower and breakfast, he headed for the bank as he had nothing to do. He would spend time reading a book, but he did not have anything to read. He reached the bank at 8:50 A.M. He hoped to spend time with the security staff or the perverted sweeper. He was surprised to find Sarma working at his desk.

Sarma welcomed Raju and said, "What is wrong with you. Don't you have anything to do? You are very early!"

"I read a book when I have time. I have no books to read. So, I came here".

"Yesterday, I put up a file to the Chief Manager for his approval. If he has already seen it, I will take the necessary action. Is he in his room? He comes early sometimes".

"I did not see"

"Will you please find out"?

Raju went to the chamber. The door has a six inch square window covered with glass, so that people can look in and see if he is free. That day it was covered with the curtain. Raju returned and said, "Curtains are drawn against the window. I could not see".

"May be he is in. Let's find out. Come with me".

They went into the room as the door was not locked. They gaped at what they saw, apologized and returned red faced.

The Chief Manager is the head of the Branch and controls all the departments of the branch. His executive chair was overloaded. Surayah was sitting on his lap. Her hands were around his neck, resting on his shoulder. His hands circled Surayah's waist and they were both happily whispering sweet nothings. They were surprised at this intrusion and broke up hastily. After sometime, Sarma was called to the Chief Manager's room.

Sarma came back and said, "He is very cool. Not embarrassed at all. He told me that he is not afraid of the disclosure of the incident. But he does not want it to be known to everybody, because that was not necessary. He told me that he would get me transferred to Koyyalagudem or any other Maoist infested areas. He wants you to meet him. There is a visitor in there. Go to him when he is alone".

After a few hours, he found the boss alone and went in. The Chief Manager instructed the duffedar not to allow anybody for some time. Raju was shown the chair.

The boss said, "You have no right to come to the bank so early. If the Union finds out, they will insist on payment of overtime".

"I was not working, Sir. I spend my time chatting with Sarma. I do not disturb him. He works and talks to me sporadically".

"I hear that you are not a gentleman either. So don't pretend to be virtuous. You know these things happen. As a man you understand, you gain nothing by talking about it. I will deny and so shall Surayah".

"She did. She wanted me to keep this secret. She explained that she tripped on a fold in the carpet and fell on you and that there was nothing between the two of you."

"That is true. I moved my chair back so that she can sweep between the chair and the table. That is how she landed on me. If the chair was not pushed back by me, she would have fallen on my right side, throwing both of us on to the floor".

"Congratulations Sir, you are still young".

"That is right boy. I haven't lost my vitality. My wife has become old and lost interest in sex".

"Seetamma told me that you have erectile dysfunction and need plenty of foreplay. When you are aroused after a lot of time, you don't last two seconds".

"She said that? That is a lie. She is saying that to protect me. What did Polamma and Mary Say?"

Raju was silent. He made no attempt to answer.

He looked at Raju in the eye and said, "You don't know?"

"No"

"Now you know".

"Yes,"

"Well that was stupid of me. I wanted the feedback".

"Seetamma may not have spoken the truth. She may be trying to tell me that you were harmless"

"Next time you meet her, tell her that if she wants pleasure, she should go to an elephant".

Raju grinned and said, "O.K."

"Do you notice that you have dropped 'Sir' when you address me?"

"I am sorry. I did not notice it sir. I do not condemn what you are doing. You must be doing yoga to retain your vigour and vitality".

"Let us talk about you for a change; you are not virtuous at all. I hear rumours about you".

"I wish they were true"

"Why? You look like a matinee idol. I am informed that girls like you".

"No. There are several risks in getting into an affair with women"

"Yes. The affairs should be casual and nothing serious should be attempted".

"That is the reason why I avoid relationship with them. I like them. So, I spend my free time with girls. They expect a relationship to develop".

"I don't know about that. Either you think that I am a fool or you are in fact a fool. With your personality and communication skills, you should be covering a lot of virgins. I am told that you are a lady killer".

"I am not Jack the Ripper"

"Well, I am Jack the Tripper".

They laughed.

Raju said, "Sarma is due for a transfer in six months. He has got everything in control. If you let him go, you may have to put up with a new incumbent, who will take a lot of time to settle down".

"You have the nerve to raise this subject now. I consider that this is blackmail".

"Nothing of the sort. I don't get an opportunity to talk to you".

"Yes, I will talk to the staff section and arrange for his retention for two more years. But, he has to leave this branch after that. He should do his mandatory rural service and has to take up business assignments".

"I do not wish to lose a good friend. You can rest assured that the matter will be kept secret".

"Thank You"

"You are lucky; we caught you in the most intimate situation with Surayah".

"Are you trying to pull my leg?"

"Normally such incidents are difficult to prove. You have two reliable witnesses. You know women. When things do not go as they wished, they scream rape or molestation and get you into trouble. Now, we know four women who have consensual sex with you. Are there any more."

"You have a point there. You also have guts to ask me for other names. You may go now. But remember that I treat you as a friend".

"Thank you, Sir"

Surayah met Raju during lunch break. She said, "You are a dumb ass. I told you that everybody wants an affair. Nobody is immune. You have not noticed because you are stupid. The dames is plumb crazy about you."

"You are trying to seduce me. If I believe you, I am sure to get in to deep trouble".

"I know that I am not good enough for you. I have no complaint. I know that I am not Miss Universe. But, you pay attention and you will understand. I have observed her face when you were talking to her. Leela is madly in love with you".

"She is too classy for me. She can get much better men than me. Besides, I want a full time house wife. I need a home and a mother of children who is devoted to us. I want her to be free to take care of children".

"Not only are you dumb, you are a century behind in your attitudes. Billions of couples work and tend to their homes. Leela is yours for the asking".

"Ah, come on".

"What is wrong with you? You are educated, handsome and well behaved. No girl has complained about you. They may not complain even if you misbehave".

"Enough of this. I have to be present at my counter".

"Remember. Everybody, I repeat, everybody. Take my word".

In the evening, Raju invited Sarma out and they were sipping tea under one of the trees in the campus. Raju said, "The laptop has been after me advising me to be promiscuous. She says that I am the most eligible bachelor and should not let go the opportunities".

"Perhaps, the laptop wants to have sex with you".

"I told her that I am not interested in her. She did not get offended. She says that I am missing the opportunities. As for herself, she says her hands are full. She says she can find time for me if I want, but there will be no hard feelings".

"I observed that Leela's cheeks turn rosy and she blushes when you pass by"

She is a working woman. I want a full time house wife with duties defined by our society".

"The traditions are changing due to exposure to Europe, U.S., etc. Your objections are irrelevant. Traditional food habits are being ignored. It has become personal choice of the individual. About 50% of every family is Non-Vegetarian and the other 50% do not touch meat even though they are traditionally non vegetarian".

"I know, my parents will accept my choice of a life partner. Even if they have some reservation, they will reconcile and agree".

"Let things develop but don't take too long"

"I spoke to the Chief Manager about your posting. At first, he thought I was seeking compensation for our silence. He later agreed to have you retained in your present assignment for two more years, when he retires".

"I admire your nerve. Thanks any way. Do not look towards your right. Laptop is passing by"

Laptop saw these two, came closer and said, "Everybody, everybody, take my word, everybody" and walked away.

Raju said, "Next time anybody says 'everybody', I am going to faint. But she is saying it out of good will. I will try to take Leela out for dinner. I will visit her parents. I will let things happen. I will take necessary action. I thought she was above my level. Nobody can fail to love her. I don't want to end up like Ravi Shankar".

"Ravi Shankar is the most eligible bachelor. When love strikes, people behave oddly. He realized his mistake after discussing with us".

"You realized your love for Leela after discussing with me and the laptop. Best of luck".

"Thank you. I will pay more attention to her and take the issue to its logical end.

THE HORSE POWER

Sarma, Raju, Sudarsan, and Chakri were sitting in an Irani restaurant chatting over tea and biscuits. That was Friday. Saturday was a holiday. With two consecutive holidays, they were discussing a short trip to Srisailam. Sudarsan said, "I can't come to Srisailam. Tomorrow evening, we are expecting some guests who are bringing marriage proposals".

"Your parents are looking for a bride for you. Is it," asked Chakri.

"No. It is for my sister. She has to be married first."

"How old is she"

"She is twenty. If things work out as we planned, she will be married when she is twenty one".

"That is the right age for marriage for girls. Men can marry by twenty five years of age".

"I feel that the age gap should not be more than three years".

"Age gap could be more. There are several successful marriages with the age gap of ten years".

"Women age faster, than men", intervened Raju.

"So what shall we do tomorrow", asked Sarma.

Chakri said, "Let us meet at 10:30 AM at the bank and decide".

"I am free till 5 PM," said Sudarsan.

"There is an officer named Venkatesam in the Advances Department. There was a complaint lodged against him with the police and the bank", said Chakri.

"It appears that he called at the house of the defaulting borrower and made advances to his wife".

"Advances Department is not for such advances".

31

"Venkatesam wants to meet me tomorrow. We will meet him and help him overcome his predicament. He is an interesting guy. Later, we can lunch at a restaurant and decide what to do".

"So the trip to Srisailam is dropped. I cannot have lunch with you guys. I should spend the holiday with my family", said Sarma.

"I will arrange for tickets to a movie for you and your family. After the movie, have dinner at a decent restaurant", suggested Raju.

"That will be fine. I will have breakfast at home and join you at the appointed hour".

"In that case, you better leave now. I shall deliver the tickets to you before 6 P.M. The ladies need some time to get ready. Inform them by phone".

"O.K. See you tomorrow", Sarma left them.

Chakri suggested, "How about spending the evening in a bar".

"That will be fine with me", said Raju.

"I am living with my parents. I cannot go home drunk", said Sudarsan.

"Nobody is getting drunk. Go home now and tell your parents that you are eating out tonight. Arrange with your sister to let you in. Are you both quite friendly and affectionate"?

"We love each other so much, she is worried about leaving us after her marriage".

"Fine. We will meet here again at 6:30 P.M. I will have to run for the movie tickets. 6:30 is ok. I can deliver the tickets, go back to my accommodation, freshen up and join you," said Raju, leaving. They broke up to meet again after an hour and quarter.

Raju was the first to arrive at the Bank next morning, followed by Sarma, then Venkatesam and Chakri. Sudarsan was a few minutes late. Sarma asked Venkatesam if everything was alright.

Venkatesam smiled and said, "If you are asking about the police complaint, the matter is closed. The Police were not inclined to pursue the matter. They were convinced that the complaint was malicious. They warned her and closed the case".

"So, what shall we do now", asked Chakri.

"I can take you to interesting places. Have you ever been to Hyderabad Race Club"?

"No". Replied the others.

"The day is taken care of. Wait in the Irani restaurant. I will borrow a car from a friend and come back to you in half an hour. There are five of us. We can go places together in a car".

He returned with a Fiat car and all of them got in. Venkatesam was driving and talking.

"One day at the Race club is not going to make you addicted to the sport. I do not recommend this to you. I am not a regular visitor. I have friends working in the Race club and one or two horse owners. That is an advantage of working in the Advances Department. We have borrowers rich enough to own race horses."

The other four listened to him in silence.

Sarma asked, "I think the first race starts at 2:00 P.M",

"Yes. We have time to do some research before we eat and go to the Race Club. We should be at the Race Club at least one hour before the first race. We have time to meet a few people, eat and be at Race Club by 1:00 P.M."

"Where are we going", asked Chakri.

"We will meet a man. He has been a regular punter for the last 40 years. His name is Satyanarayana. He worked in Accountant General's office and retired recently. He lives in Chikkadapalli," explained Venkatesam.

Satyanarayana was tall, slim with a pointed nose and long, thin face and plenty of grey hair. He did not look his age. He welcomed the group pleasantly.

"Venky, you brought the entire staff. What a pleasure," he said addressing the group, "I am Satayanarayana and it is lovely to meet you. Come in. Would you like to have some coffee. Please sit down".

The others introduced themselves. Sarma said, "I see that you are studying the Punters' book. I hope we are not disturbing you".

"Yes, I am going through this book. This small book contains the entire information on the races today, racing time, the horses running, their record in the previous races, the pedigree, the handicap, the names of their owners, trainers etc. It also gives the names of horses that are likely to win in the races. This is an encyclopaedia for the punters.

Venkatesam said, "My friends are all new to racing. I don't think they are interested. I brought them along as we met".

"That's how anybody enters this sport. Some are drawn to it and it becomes an obsession, just as it did to me".

"They are not likely to be addicted".

"But, let them place a couple of bets. There is the beginner's luck. They watch the horses in the paddock and select the horse that bucks, snickers or salivates and so on and place a bet on it and win".

"But, you have been betting on horses for the last forty years. You may be able to choose the winner. After all these years, how is your position. Have you made big profits", asked Sarma.

"No, I have not made a killing so far. I just about break even, give or take a few thousand rupees".

"You must have already made up your mind about the horses that are likely to win", asked Venkatesam.

"I have selected a few horses, but I take the decision only a few minutes before the commencement of the race".

"Can you give us any tips?"

"Sure, why not".

He gave them the options for all the five races of the day. They talked about racing, politics, movies etc., for some time and took leave of him.

Venkatesam said, "I told you about the horse owners in our books. I made arrangement for five passes to the Member's Enclosure. We will collect them at the Race club. Now, I will take you to another exceptional punter. His approach to forecasting a winner is singular. Do not snigger. He is quite serious. He drove them to a place in Asok Nagar. The house is big and has a large Veranda. There are already six people there.

When the owner of the house saw this group, he smiled and welcomed them.

"I see you have brought some of your colleagues. Are they regular punters?"

"No. This is the first time for them. I want them to win a few lakhs".

"Good. Let them not bet heavily. It is not the question of merely winning. They should enjoy the sport."

Venkatesam introduced his friends to Subrahmanyam, the owner of the house.

"Are you a regular race enthusiast" asked Sarma.

"I never miss a race day. I don't consider it as gambling but as a sport. My wife says that I am giving it some respectability but it is undoubtedly gambling. Every man has got his weakness".

"Have you selected the winners today"?

"I am in the process of selecting. I study the horses and also study their chances of winning through Astrology. The horoscopes of each of the horses are drawn and we attempt to forecast their performance. The winning horses are predicted on the basis of planetary position at the time of the race".

"That will take a lot of time as there will be at least fifty to sixty horses running on each race day".

"Yes. We select one or two races only. Drawing horoscope charts for each of the horses is tedious".

"You should know the place, date and time of birth of each of the horses to draw their horoscopes".

"There are several ways of drawing the horoscopic charts".

The astrologer who is the brother of Subrahmanyam, the master of the house announced, "Sea Breeze has the best chances of winning in the second race. The Black Horse is set to win in the fourth race".

Subrahmanyam said, "There you are. You got tips for two races. Your guess is as good as mine for the other three races".

Sarma asked the Astrologer, "How can you predict a winning horse without having the details of its birth".

"We consider the time of the race and planetary configuration at that time, its influence on my brother and the horses. If we get fair analysis, we make a prediction. I am not very proficient in this subject, but my friend here, is".

Sarma appreciated their innovative method. Subrahmanyam explained, "I made a couple of killings on the strength of their prediction. I don't ignore their forecast".

"How much do they charge you for their prediction"?

"Nothing. They are interested in the races too. They are also regular punters".

"You make a killing when the prediction is correct, but you must be losing heavily, when their prediction fails".

"I have a ceiling for the bet. I never bet more than Rs.10, 000 at a time. When I won, it was when the odds are approximately 30 to 1. So, I am always on the plus side".

"That is sensible".

Venkatesam said, "Let's go. They have to make preparations for today's events".

They took leave of the Subrahmanyam and company and went to a restaurant. Venkatesam said, "We had a very interesting time today, is it not".

All of them agreed.

After lunch, they proceeded to the Race club. It was 12:30 PM. Venkatesam drove towards Malakpet. Almost all the vehicles were headed towards the Race Club. All the drivers and passengers were riding with serious anticipation and determination on their faces. All of them were holding the small racing booklets. All the passengers were studying the booklets with concentration. They appeared to have taken decision about the horses to be backed and leave a little leeway for last minute changes.

They arrived at the Race club about five minutes before One 'O' clock. They collected the passes and the badges for the member's enclosure. Venkatesam guided them to the paddock and asked them to be seated, while he went in search of somebody. The four of them watched the horses for the first race being shown. The horses were led by the syces. The horses were nearly six feet high and were beautiful. They realized that there is a good reason to fall in love with racing. Venkatesam returned about 01:15 P.M. The horses in the paddock were being paraded with the jockeys mounted on them.

Venkatesam said, "I have an excellent tip. I know that you cannot be convinced if I merely name the horse. But it is such a closely guarded secret. You should not divulge this information before the race and after for at least five years. I am perhaps the world's biggest ass to share the secret with the four of you. I might as well grab a mike and announce it".

Sarma said, "We are holding several secrets and one more cannot be a problem. You can safely trust us".

"This is a very heavy secret and I am so excited about it that I cannot hold it. I told you that some of our borrowers own horses. During my inspections, I met a man named Somayya who is the Chief Syce with trainer RS Nayudu. He is trainer for the horses of one of our borrowers. Let me caution you again. If this secret leaks out, the reprisals would be heavy".

"Rest assured. It won't be leaked by us".

"Well, I take your word for it. The borrower owns a stable of horses".

Sunshine and Moonshine are owned by him. All his horses are trained by Nayudu. They are both chocolate brown and look alike.

All horses look alike to me except for the colour," commented Sudarsan.

"I have been pestering him for a tip for the last one year. He confided in me today. It is a tip of lifetime.

"We are holding our breath. Please go on", said Chakri.

"It is in the third race. The horse is Moonshine. This cannot fail. Please do not bet in any other race. Save whatever money you have for the third race".

"There is nothing confidential about this. Such tips are dime a dozen", commented Raju.

"The secret is the way the horse is maneuvered. Moonshine is in excellent form. It won at Bombay this season and is moved to class 1".

"I read the booklets and it is in poor form in Hyderabad, You can see it in the book now", said Sarma.

"Exactly, The Race club allotted number 436 to Moonshine and 634 to Sunshine. They switched the numbers".

"Oh! My God! That is dangerous and is a fraud".

"That is the reason why it should be kept secret".

"Aren't there any checks"

"There are. But they somehow managed it. We are not involved. We follow the tip".

"So, what happened"?

"The press, the club and other commentators were fooled".

"Be clear man".

"You see, when the numbers are switched, Moonshine gets the Sunshine timings in the practice runs. Sunshine is in poor form, but gets the Moonshine timings which are excellent. So, the Moonshine with Sunshine record is rated poor and is an outsider. It is in the third race with very low profile. Sunshine is not running in this race. Moonshine is in the race and is expected to rank 'also ran' category, but can win the race by walking. Moonshine is identified by its correct number today."

The group spent their time eating peanuts and drinking tea and gossiping till the end of the second race. They watched the horses paraded in the paddock and went to the Bookie's enclosure.

Hard Core is the favourite in the third race. Black Knight was the next favourite. Hard Core was quoted at 9/10 and Black Knight at 2 to 1. Moonshine opened at 30 to 1. After fifteen minutes, Moonshine was quoted at 20 to 1.Heavy betting was done in favour of the Moonshine with all the bookies.

Venkatesam said, "There is heavy betting on Moonshine by vested interests. Let us wait for some more time".

After sometime Moonshine's odds were raised to 30 to 1. There was further betting and it was quoted 25 to 1. Sudarsan said, "I have Rs2000. If we win, my sister's marriage is financed".

Venkatesam said, "Everyman for himself in betting. Let there be no syndicating. The odds are now back to 30 to 1"

"Shall we bet now," asked Raju?

"Let us wait for few minutes. There is a last minute change. The notified jockey Sahadev is dropped as he is indisposed with fever and did not arrive from Madras. The new jockey is Ahmed".

"Does it change the course of event," asked Sarma.

"I talked to Somayya. He says all that the jockey has to do is to start promptly and take care not to fall from the horse. The people with the vested interest have invested heavily with the bookies as we have seen. With the change announced, the odds were further raised to 35 to 1. Let's bet now. Let each of us go to different bookies".

Sarma invested Rs.2000, Chakri Rs.3000, Raju Rs.500 and Venkatesam Rs.10000.

Venkatesam said, "This is an opportunity of life time. I would have been happier if Sahadev were to ride because he did practice on the horse".

They went to the gallery and took seats near the finish line. The horses were at the starting gate and one by one they were entering their stalls. All the horses were in the starting stalls. At exactly the scheduled time, the starters' bell rang and the starting gates were open

All the horses jumped from their gates and were running as a bunch. Moonshine did not start. Hard Core was at the head of the bunch together with two others. Ten meters passed and there was no sign of Moonshine. When the pack reached 20 meters, White wonder and Black Knight were in the lead. Moonshine jumped from the starting gate and was running. But a lead of 30 meters cannot be overcome. Adrenaline pumped into their heads, they were hot with rising temperature.

"We were screwed. It is impossible to catch up with the bunch of high speed horses with such a lead".

At 100 meters mark, Moonshine was several lengths behind and lead bunch was nowhere near. At 500 meters mark, Moonshine reduced the gap, but was still several lengths behind. From the gallery, the horses appeared to be gliding. Moonshine was giving its best. The group of bankers were staring at the racing horses. Their faces were hot, their tongues dry and the adrenaline that was being pumped made their body temperature high. They were sweating.

At 1000 meter mark, Moonshine caught up with the pack. The bankers were screaming encouragement to Moonshine. The horse didn't care. It was running at tremendous speed. 1200 meter mark, Moonshine was the last of the pack on the outside. Turning the bend at 1400 meter mark, Moonshine was in the fourth place, but Hard Core was leading by two lengths followed by Love Light and Black Knight. Moonshine was one length behind the pack, but was running on the outside. Last 100 meters, it was at the tail of the leader. Moonshine was running for its life. Last 20 meters, the horses could be seen. Moonshine was galloping at high speed, its head bobbing and eyes glassy. The jockey was standing on the stirrups, bent forward, head & shoulder bent encouraging Moonshine to run faster by brushing its rump with the whip. The horses passed the bankers. Grassy chunks of earth were kicked high in to the air by the hooves of the running horses. They flashed past with Moonshine behind Hard Core by a neck. All the people in the gallery were standing and screaming for their favourite horses. The horses reached the finish line. Moonshine was on the level with the Hard Core while the rest of the pack was a length behind.

"There comes the light. It is a photo finish"

The feverish pitch of the commentator's voice was silent.

After agonizing minutes of wait, the mike announced, "It's Hard Core, Hard Core won the race by a whisker".

The group was silent for a few minutes trying to return to normal.

Venkatesam commented with a disappointed smile, "That is racing for you".

Sarma said, "What a race. Moonshine ran with such a speed, it appeared to be gliding".

"If the Moonshine started a second early, we would have won handsome dividends," said Raju.

They lost interest in the other races and were walking towards the car, when they came across Somayya, who was in tears.

"I cannot afford to lose. The inexperienced jockey ruined the race".

"You cannot anticipate last minute hurdles. Do not lose heart".

"I have not only lost my heart, but also a lot of money".

"Don't give up hope. We will try to do better in future. I will be in touch with you. We will win," said Venkatesam, passing Rs 2000 to him.

THE THREE PACK

Syam was one of the new recruits. He belongs to the batch of Raju. Within a few months of their appointment, Chakri was engaged to be married. Syam felt that Chakri was lucky to find his girl in the Bank. He did not expect that staff marrying another employee is possible as they were total strangers. He was surprised that Raju was spending more time with Leela. He noticed that Leela was responding to Raju's attention. If Raju marries Leela, it would be the second marriage between the colleagues. Syam was 5'6" in height, light brown in colour and had the look of a man with a serious purpose.

Syam and Raju were sharing the same table in the canteen that day. Syam commented that, "In this Bank job, we get very little physical exercise. We tend to accumulate a lot of fat around the waist".

Raju agreed, "Yes. You are right. We walk or play games in the evening, but that is not enough".

"What games do we play? After Bank, we gather in a room and play cards. That is worse than Banking, where we walk from one desk to another to pass on the papers".

Raju agreed and said, "We are at least worried about lack of exercise. The girls are much worse. They pay lot of attention to their faces and ignore the rest of the body. After a few years, their waist line is covered by flab like cycle tyres set one over the other".

"Do you exercise?"

"I practice the martial arts. I am trained and keep myself in good health. Otherwise I will be beaten thoroughly in the work outs and sparring sessions".

"Good for you. I am thinking of taking suitable precautions and do exercise that suits me".

They were joined by Kamal. Kamal was recruited under sports quota. He was a football player. He played for the nationals and represented the state. The Bank has a full team of football players. Kamal plays at the right back and defends excellently.

He said, "If you want exercises, join us at 6:00 AM at the stadium".

"That is too rigorous. Besides you are allowed to leave at 3:30 PM for practice. I have a few ideas. I will try them".

Kamal said, "The Bank job makes us lazy. Whenever there is a match, we have players who complain of back ache, sprained ankles and so on. The great blaming game is played in the dressing room after every match".

"If you stop playing, you will be required to work full time in the Bank," said Raju.

"What is the problem? Football is not given equal priority. Cricketers enjoy more benefits. We have two players who played in the Test Matches. After one or two tests, they were dropped from the national team. But they do not attend the Bank regularly".

"Cricket is popular. Cricketers are treated as heroes," said Syam.

Raju said, "In England, where cricket is born, soccer is more popular than cricket. We, in India, look down upon any other game".

They finished lunch and returned to their places of work. Raju became more attached to Leela. He realized that he was deeply in Love with her. He was surprised at such strong emotion for Leela. It did not strike him until others pointed it out.

Sarma commented one day, "Syam is very strong. When you shake hands with him, his grip is so strong and his hand shake so powerful, that all the organs in your body vibrate for a few seconds".

"Syam is a physical fitness fad," said Raju.

'He does not have to be strong. Some light exercise would be adequate to maintain good health".

"Syam is not aiming for championship in weight lifting or wrestling or body building. Is he?"

"No. He is only interested in keeping fit".

"Animals, birds etc. run or fly as soon as they get up. I don't think they suffer from high cholesterol or irregular B.P or diabetes. Man wakes up, moves from the bed to sofa and reads the newspaper over a cup of bed coffee. I should also do some exercises," said Sarma.

"When do you propose to start? There will be body pains for about fifteen days," said Raju.

"After fifteen days. I am going for Vasectomy next week. I will take rest and start exercising slowly".

"You don't need fifteen days' rest. It is as simple as clipping the nails," said Raju.

"How do you know?"

"I heard people say so".

"I am eligible for a special leave of one week. Why should I forego that privilege"?

Syam said, "Wish you all the best and speedy recovery".

"I am going to the doctor next week. There is time for the best wishes"

"I know. I do not know if I will meet you next week".

"In that case, thank you"

"Syam, you do not need rippling muscles to stay fit. People can see your muscles only after you take off your shirt and vest".

"I know. I will find something suitable".

One week later, Raju and Sudarsan visited Sarma at his house. He was sterilized a few hours back. Sarma greeted them happily.

"I am glad you have come".

"How did the surgery go," asked Raju.

"It was a simple operation. But, I suffered discomfort before the operation"

"What is that"?

"That hospital has a 12' x 12' store room. All the antiseptics, surgical equipment, cotton rolls, gauze and other items are stored. At the centre of the room, there is long table where the patients lie. The patients are prepared for surgery".

"That must be a rented place. Hospitals in their own building have pre-operative rooms".

"I was asked to take off my clothes and lie on the table. Even the briefs are to be taken off. You should lie naked. I complied with the requirement. The attendant who guided me to the room asked me to wait and left. Nurses, attendants, doctors etc. were coming in for surgical material, medicines etc., and going out. The door was never closed. Nobody was looking at me but a lot of people were coming in and going out. There were post-operative, ante natal care rooms opposite to the room. People walking by were looking at the body on the table".

"That must be embarrassing," said Sudarsan.

"That is the understatement of the year. After five minutes, which felt like an hour, the attendant came with a barber's knife. He shaved six inches above and six inches below the area of surgery on my body. He cleaned the area with spirit or an antiseptic and went out. I felt naked".

"You were naked already"

"I felt more naked. The attendant returned and covered me with some kind of apron which was open at the back and was moved to operation theatre. There were two doctors, one of them a lady, and two nurses present in the room. The words 'everybody' was ringing in my ears. I was terribly worried that I might be aroused if the lady doctor or the nurse touched me. That was unnecessary as I was injected with local anaesthesia. I did not feel any pain but I heard the sizzling noise of soldering rod touching something soft like skin or nerve".

"That is called cauterizing. The blood vessels are sealed with a soldering iron to prevent bleeding and infection," said Raju.

"How do you know?"

"There is a doctor in our family"

"They sutured the incision and covered it with bandage. I was moved to a room. Half an hour later, I was discharged and asked to return after four days".

All of them laughed at this episode. Raju said, "We miss you in the Bank".

"You can come to my house daily and spend some time".

He looked at Sudarsan and said, "I understand your emotion during the medical examination at the time of your appointment".

Sudarsan smiled and said, "Thank you. That experience still rattles me".

"Take rest for fifteen days and commence yoga or any other helpful physical activity".

Syam and Chakri complained that they were not informed about the visit to Sarma's house.

Sudarsan said, "It is only Vasectomy and not a heart attack. You were not available at the time".

Syam announced that his parents are looking for marriage alliance. But he was not thinking of marriage for a few months.

"Why do you want to wait for a few months? You have a job and can take care of your family" asked Sudarsan.

"I have my reasons. I will tell you at an appropriate time. Sudarsan, why don't you marry?"

"I have a sister. She should be married first".

"How old is she"

"She is twenty. She will complete her post graduate examination before her twenty first birthday."

"Are you looking for suitable and eligible bachelors?"

"Yes"

Chakri said, "I have saved my parents the trouble of searching for a bride"

"When is the marriage?"

"In June, this year".

"Raju's marriage will also be in June at the speed he is moving".

"Raju is hopelessly in love with Leela. She can get better offers from rich and highly gifted bachelors".

Raju said, "I know one such proposal. The boy was handsome, rich, has engineering degree from an Indian University and an MBA from the Boston University. His father has a lot of factories, business and land. He fell in love with Leela at first sight. Despite his education, he lost his mind and behaved oddly".

"What are your chances of success with that kind of competition?"

"Nil. But I love her so much that I am afraid that I will behave badly".

"Don't think negatively. Several of our colleagues are madly in love with her"

"I will settle the matter soon"

"Best of luck," said Syam and others.

Sarma returned to work. Raju and Sudarsan were happy.

Raju asked, "Is everything ok?"

"Yes, that is a very minor surgery. Some incident spoiled the mood".

"What is it?"

"The attendant left me naked in a busy place. The unpleasant situation could have been avoided"

Raju said, "Welcome back"

"Thank you. Did you meet the Chief Manager, when I was on leave?"

"No, I do not report to him on my own. I will only report to my supervisor"

"What is the matter involving the Chief Manager," asked Syam.

"It is about a note put up to him. Raju went to him and explained the matter to the Chief Manager".

One day Sarma asked Raju.

"I am ready to begin my exercises. I will start from tomorrow. Can you accompany me?"

"Oh! Yes. First, start with the brisk walk. We can move to other exercises gradually."

"Walking is not enough?"

"It will control Cholesterol. You will be fresh and relaxed".

After a few days, Raju said, "We will now commence running"

"Running? That will be too much for me".

"Initially it will be difficult. After two or three weeks, the aches and pain will disappear and you will enjoy running. It burns calories and make you feel light. Now commence jogging"

Sarma ran for a few meters and asked, "Is that ok".

"You are not jogging. You are kicking the ground. Let the leg move forward, take a slightly longer step. You should learn to copy the dog trot".

"Thank you".

"You try to practice some Yoga Asanas(postures). Learn them from a teacher. Do not do them on your own"

"Why don't you teach me?"

"I do not practice Yoga. I am not competent to teach"

One day, they found Syam sitting on a bench on the Tank Bund. They did not talk to him until their trot is completed.

Raju asked, "Syam, why are you sitting alone. You look worried."

"I have my problems".

"If you have a problem, you should share it with your friends. May be we can help".

"I have to go to a girl's house to see her and at the same time she can see me. This is a marriage proposal"

"So, what is the problem"?

"I don't want to go. I don't want to marry for a few more months"

"Have you heard something bad about her or her family?"

"No. That is not the issue. The girl is said to be pretty"

"The horoscopes do not match?"

"We have no such practice in our family."

"What is the problem then? You can always decline the alliance after seeing the girl"

"That would be cruel. If she is pretty, I do not want to decline the offer"

Sarma intervened and said, "Your behaviour is odd and there is something wrong with you. If you like the girl, marry her".

"If I have to marry this girl, I want the nuptials after three or four months"

"This is strange. These days, people are asking for anticipatory Nuptials. You have a problem".

"My father is worried. He thinks that I am not normal. My mother says I am acting like a nut. She wants me take a thorough medical examination to ensure that I am normal. She also wants me to consult a shrink".

"No doubt that they have a reason to worry. You are acting mysteriously"

"There is no mystery. I will explain everything this evening. Come to my house at 6:00 PM. I have a room for myself. We can sit there and talk".

"They dispersed and reassembled in the evening at Syam's house. Syam's parents were glad to receive them. They expressed their displeasure and worry on account of Syam's behavior. They went into Syam's room and were about to start talking about Syam's predicament.

Syam said, "Sh . . . Wait for a few minutes. My mother will bring some coffee and snacks"

The guests looked around the room and were impressed as the room was clean and neatly arranged. The breeze from the windows was cool and relaxing. There were some sports equipment like Dumbbells, Bull Worker etc.

Sarma asked, "Syam, do you use the Bull Worker. It is an isometric exercise"

Syam's mother came in carrying a large tray containing snacks, coffee and water in a glass mug.

She said, "Put some sense into his mind. I am disappointed with him. He is not a man".

"Amma, that is a cruel thing to say" screamed Syam.

She left the room without a glance at him.

Syam explained, "That Bull Worker is the problem. I have always admired the athletes with rippling muscles. I wanted a six pack".

"What are you going to do with the six pack. You will have to take off your clothes for others to see your six pack. Now that you have already commenced the exercises, continue"

"My tragedy is that I have only three pack despite my best efforts"

"What is a three pack? I have heard of six pack and eight pack".

Syam removed his shirt and the vest. All of them stared at the body. It has in fact only three pack.

"I worked on the Bull Worker. It works. But, in my case it created a problem."

"We don't use the left hand as much as the right hand. There is disuse of the left hand"

"Exactly, when I used the Bull Worker, the right hand was exerting pressure, while the left hand had no pressure. So, the muscles on the right side are fully developed. The left hand side of the body was plain. Not a single muscle".

"As a result, you have the half of the six pack as the left side was plain. So, the right side has three pack and the other three pack did not develop on the left".

"I have stopped using that contraption and am waiting for the ripples on the right side to melt and the body becomes plain equally on both sides"

"You have a problem, I admit. Why should this stop your marriage? The lady would be surprised, no doubt. But she will understand your problem. This is not a permanent disability. I am quite sure that she will enjoy the available three pack".

Raju suggested, "Even if you agree to the marriage, it will take three to four months for it to take place. By then, you will become plain all over".

Sudarsan said, "It is quite rare to find half developed body. Do not stop your parents. Let them go ahead with their arrangements"

"But, I will not tell them about my experience with Isometrics".

"That is up to you. If you tell them, they will help you and encourage you".

All of them went down and introduced themselves to Syam's parents.

"Do you understand his problem? We are thoroughly disappointed with him".

"He has no problem, sir. He just wants to enjoy the bachelorhood for a few more months".

"What is there to enjoy in the life of a bachelor. Marriage can be enjoyed. The partner in his life would make his life a pleasant experience"

"He agrees, Sir. You can look for alliances"

Surprised, his father asked Syam, "Is that true. Shall we go ahead with the search for bride?"

Syam replied, "As you wish, Nanna"

Syam's father asked, "What was the problem? We have been discussing with him the marriage proposals. We could not get him to see the reason. Within few minutes, you solved problem. What is all this about?"

"Nothing. He wanted to marry after he passed the Banking institute's exam. We told him that marriage will not come in the way of his studies".

"Thank you. I hope we do not have any more problems with him".

"There will be no more problems".

Syam had come out to see them off. At the gate, Sarma advised, "There are always two sides to any situation. One is positive and the other is negative. If you look at the positive side of the problem, you become an optimist and successful. You have been looking at the negative side of it and ruining your peace of mind".

Syam replied happily, "Thank you. You have made my problem disappear. This is a small matter. I made a mountain of it. I feel relieved and jubilant".

He was smiling when he said, "good night".

On the way home, Sarma said, "A positive outlook saves us from worry and unhappiness. For instance, the Superintendent at the hospital commented that I have a small scrotum. I told him that I am happy with what I got"

Sudarsan said, "Some people who were born in traditional vegetarian families are said to have small scrotum. It does not affect your sexual powers. It makes no difference".

Raju said, "That Superintendent had no business to talk like that. A big scrotum is no advantage. In fact, it is a liability. It is luggage and such people cannot cross their legs when they are sitting"

"You should thank God for his creation. There should be no whining. Make the best of what you are given by him".

Syam was all smiles when he reported for work next day. He said, "You made me look at the positive side of the situation. I am now confident and optimistic. After all, the problem is not serious and will be solved without any effort. Patience is the answer".

Raju said," My situation also requires a positive approach. I have one advantage over Ravi Shankar. I know the girl and am quite friendly with her. Ravi Shankar could not approach her and express his intentions. That is what made him desperate. So he behaved like he did despite his talent. My problem is that I know her. That makes things difficult for me. I cannot take a 'no' from her. As far as we know, she declined nearly one hundred people."

"It is already decided. You cannot escape from your fate," Sarma said.

"It is very difficult to select a wife. I do not believe that love marriages are a great success. They have their own problems. There are many broken homes".

"Arranged marriages have their own advantages and disadvantages. Parents look at all possible angles and select the bride or bride groom. Long association with the spouse can lead to love".

"I remember Raju saying that he would not recognize love when it strikes him. Remarks from the colleagues made him realize it. Now, he is so much in Love that he cannot behave normally," said Syam.

Raju said, "The positive factors are Leela and I belong to the same community, I am quite friendly with her. She is about my own age. I don't think that is a negative factor. The major hurdle is the horoscope. Both the families are particular about it. I want a full time house wife. But as Sarma said, the times have changed. After this analysis, I don't know what to do".

"Propose to her and break the suspense".

"I am trying to muster the courage to do that. I would have done that already, but if she declines, I may not marry anybody else. I will remain a bachelor".

Syam applied for permission to leave early as he and his family, are going to a girl's house to see the bride. Chakri, Sudarsan, Raju and Sarma wished him the best of luck. The girl's parents were waiting to receive them. Next day, Syam recounted the events to his friends.

"They were waiting for us. We were given a cool welcome".

"Cool welcome? That is bad," said Chakri.

"India is warm country. Cool welcome means good welcome. Warm welcome is positive in the west, where the temperature is low".

"I got your point. We ape the westerners and consider a warm welcome is good and respectable"

"Cool Welcome is comfortable and respectable" said Sarma.

"The girl is very attractive. I liked her instantly and whispered the same thing to my mother".

"Can't you wait until we go home," she hissed.

"The bride's father asked me and the girl to go to a room to talk to each other. We talked for ten minutes and came out."

"What did you talk about," asked Chakri.

"Oh! This and that I do not remember most of it."

Sarma intervened, "Chakri that is not proper to ask him for such details. They spoke to each other."

"My mother gave the fruits, flowers and sweets to the girl and put a kumkum dot on her forehead. We did not touch any of the sweets and snacks. We accepted the coffee".

Sarma said, "It is believed that if you eat at the time, the marriage will not take place".

"The girl's parents rang us up and enquired about my opinion. As I have already given my consent, they are proceeding to make arrangements. The girl called me today and spoke for some time. I told her that I will call her whenever I am free. In both of our houses, nobody is lifting the phone when it rings. It is for me or her to find out who the caller was".

"Congratulations," said Raju.

Syam invited them to tea in the neighbourhood Irani Restaurant. They assembled at the Irani restaurant that evening. Syam announced, "The wedding is fixed for 11th May".

"That is only two weeks from now," said Chakri.

"Yes. Marriage halls are not available in June, July or August."

"But the muscles will not melt in two weeks".

"I am not worried. I am glad I discussed the matter with you. I am not concerned about that now. Sudha and I are planning our honeymoon"

"It's Sudha now".

"Her parents are arranging accommodation in Horsely Hills for fifteen days".

"Where is the wedding?" asked Sarma

"In Secunderabad. Two days after marriage, we go to Horsely Hills for our honeymoon. Sarma garu, I need leave for three weeks in May".

"That is the season for vacation. Schools will be closed for summer and most of the families go on tour or visit their parents".

"What should I do now?"

"You will be granted leave, whatever the situation is. How can we refuse leave for your marriage and after?"

Syam's wedding was a grand affair. There were the traditional Mridangam and Sannayi in carnatic music. In the twin cities, the band of about 7 or 8 people performing is a must. The wedding was at 8:18 p.m. The food was delicious, only problem was the distance. That did not deter the visitors. It never did for any marriage. That is a once in a lifetime affair.

Syam and his wife arrived at Horsely Hills about 5:30 PM and were shown to their cottage. They ate pakodis and had coffee. They went out for a walk and returned about 8:00 P.M. The weather was pleasant and comfortable. Food was ready on the table. The Pundit (priest) instructed them that nuptials has to take place after 8:26 PM. They spent some time chatting and took shower. They entered the bedroom. Both were embarrassed about sleeping on the same bed. They were anxious and tense.

Syam broke the silence and asked her, "How would you like a man. Do you prefer a man with rippling muscles or a flat torso"?

"What is the point in asking now? I am your wife. I like you as you are. If you are muscular and strong, I like you. If you are flat and strong, I like you. Can't you think of anything better to talk about"?

"You express your preference and you will get it".

"Don't be silly. Stop talking about it. You are my husband and I agreed to marry you without looking at your naked torso or any other part. If you still persist in such nonsense, take a pillow and sleep on the sofa in the hall."

Syam said, "We are fighting already. I don't want a fight on the first night of our marriage. I am sorry"

He took off his shirt and the vest. She stared at him and said, "I really do have a choice. You are giving me a sample of both the options. I am sorry that I did not understand, even though no bride will tolerate such talk".

"I am sorry. I did not know how to explain to you".

"How did you manage to get into this shape?"

Syam explained the story of his three pack.

"I think I like you flat and strong. We are going to live together for the next forty to fifty years or more. I crave your love and expect you to treat me well"

"I will do as you wish. I promise."

FIRST BLOOD

"This is Sarma, my Supervisor and a friend. Sarma garu, this is my father" introduced Sudarsan.

Sarma had just returned from lunch with Raju. Sudarsan called Raju and introduced him to his father.

"Happy to meet you, sir. We have been planning to visit you".

"You are welcome anytime. Please give me a ring before you start", said Sudarsan's dad.

"We have Sudarsan. He will take care of the things. I am told that you are building a house in Ashok Nagar. How is the progress"?

"The basic structure was constructed in no time. But, the plastering, sanitary fitting, electrical work, flooring etc. take a very long time. Three fourths of the work is completed. I have come to invite you to the Grihapravesam on Friday"

"We have two days. You said that the house is not complete".

"Normally Grihapravesam is performed before the house is completed. That is the normal tradition. Another reason is that we will be ready to move into the new house. We do not have to wait for the Muhurtam"

"How is your health, sir?"

"It is ok, but for the age related atrophy in the knees, eyes, ears etc."

Sarma laughed and said, "You have covered almost all of your body".

Sudarsan's father grinned and said, "It starts with abnormal blood pressure, then raising level of cholesterol, arthritis and so on. You are all very young. You cannot understand these problems".

"Why don't you start exercising"?

"I tried walking for a few days. When the doctor advised me to walk in the morning, I was very enthusiastic. I bought special shoes for walking, shorts, T-shirts and a stick. I walked for a few days and decided to take rest for one day. I am still resting. It has been nearly four months".

"We will be glad to come to the ceremony if it is not during the Banking hours".

"It is at 11:15 A.M".

"In that case, we will call on you after you moved in to the new house. I heard that the Pancha Karma or Kaya Kalpa treatments in the Kerala Ayurveda hospitals cure Rheumatism and other diseases. Why don't you try them?"

"I will," said the man and bid goodbye to them.

A few minutes before the lunch break, Leela came to Raju and asked, "Have you seen the movie Sankarabharanam. That is a musical cinema with lot of carnatic music. You don't have to take music lessons to see that movie".

Raju replied, "No. I will go one of these days. I need company. Sarma cannot come because he has to take his family. Chakri and Syam are engaged and are dating their fiancés. I am left with Sudarsan. We will go when he is free. Do you enjoy carnatic music?"

"I practice carnatic vocal every morning. That is my prayer. All Keertanas are prayers".

"That is why your voice is so sweet. Why don't you go for auditions to All India Radio and cinemas"?

"I will go when I feel like it. For me, it is prayer. I am not interested in commercial singing at the moment"

"What is wrong with that? You have talent. It should be available to the society"

"If you have commercial interest, you crave applause, media recognition and want to become a celebrity. You deviate from the primary objective. I was requested by the music societies and have performed in three or four concerts. The original purpose of devotion is lost. I will take the opportunities that come to me. I don't want the competition singing".

"Your parents must have given you the direction of purpose"

"Yes. My family supports my attitude. Tumbura, Narada, Purandara Dasa, Thyagaraja, Annamaya and hundreds of other singers used music as medium for prayers"

"Do not decline when the opportunity comes to you".

"These days, concerts of carnatic music have an audience of twenty or thirty people. If you sing 'Mustafa ya Mustafa' it will be house full. I do not want to dishonour the carnatic music by singing to uninterested audience.

I will continue to practice and preserve the heritage. Tamilians are more appreciative"

"Well, you have the clarity of purpose. Congratulations".

"It is time for lunch. My friends will be waiting in the canteen"

Kamal, the football player had come to the group consisting of Sarma, Raju, Sudarsan and others. He said, "There is friendly match between our team and the Assam Rifles on Saturday at 4 PM. Would any of you be interested in watching and supporting us"?

Chakri and Syam said that they have other engagements. The other three agreed.

"You should be ready to start at 2:30 PM sharp. Otherwise the light will be poor in the second half."

Sudarsan said, "I will be ready. Don't forget to take me with you".

Sarma and Raju agreed to be ready at 2:30 PM. Sarma commented, "Sudarsan, I did not know that you are so interested in football".

"I like football. I go to the tournaments and matches. There is another reason for my interest in this match"

"What is that?"

"As you are aware, we are looking for a match to my sister. Yesterday, we discussed a proposal. My parents are interested and are planning to approach that family. The boy is Capt. Mohan in Assam Rifles. As the Bank's team plays against Assam Rifles on Saturday. I will get an opportunity to see him".

On Saturday, a military truck arrived at the Bank promptly at 2:00 PM. The team and its three supporters boarded the truck at 2:30 PM and arrived at the football ground in the cantonment near Langar House. There were several cottages lined up in U shape and a large football field, Basketball and Volleyball courts and still has a lot of ground left free. At the central cottage of line of cottages is the Brigadier's office. Exactly four cottages were on both sides of the Brigadier's office, which is facing the entire open space of nearly 15 acres. Military truck driver had little respect for the local traffic and the police. At one intersection, the red light was on. He didn't care. He jumped the red light, but was stopped by the vehicles obeying the green light. The Military Police sitting next to the driver got down and signalled the traffic to stop. Nobody stopped and the policeman objected. He aimed his machine gun at the vehicles, which stopped promptly. The Army truck moved on and the MP jumped on the foot board and returned to his seat.

Sudarsan commented, "They have little respect for the civilians and the Police. We do not see the Army personnel in public, so we do not know the attitude".

"They have contempt for the civilians, the police etc. Bankers are considered vegetables with large bottoms and blown out bellies", said Sarma.

"They don't trust the politicians but humour them and treat them with the pretence of respect because they are the ruling class"

"Why so?" asked Sudarsan.

"Bankers are white collar workers pushing paper. Police duty is control of law & order, crime and traffic. Army is a combat force. They engage in combat at the orders of the superior officer without question. The discipline is awesome compared to the civilian arguments and dissent".

The Bank's team was received my Major Subba. Refreshments were ready on a table. Cakes, biscuits, hot tea, water, paper plates and cups were placed on the long table. After the refreshments, the team members were introduced to the Colonel, who came to watch the friendly match. Capt. Mohan was not present. The match started at exactly 4:00 PM. The military team was playing like a well-oiled machine. The army players were well disciplined and were not talking. The Bank's players were calling to the players with the possession of the ball. Sarma said the calls for the ball were to indicate the position of the caller as the man with the ball may not have the time to search for the available team mate.

Forty minutes into the first half, the Bank's right winger had dribbled the ball through the right flank and passed it on to the centre forward who kicked the ball powerfully in to the goal. The Army goal keeper blocked the ball, but could not hold it. The rebound was kicked into the goal by the on rushing striker from the Bank. At half time, the score was one goal lead by the Bankers.

In the second half, there was heavy pressure from the silently playing Army team. The ball was in possession of the army most of the time. The Bank team's defence was tested severely. At the 85th minute, the Army forward had taken the ball to the left flank and passed it on like drawing minus into the penalty area. The ball was intercepted by George, the left back but was overwhelmed by the on rushing forwards of the Army. George could not hold on to the ball and kicked it back to the goal keeper. The Bank's goal keeper was not expecting this move and the ball sailed into the net. After 90 minutes, the score was 1-1. The match was a draw.

Colonel Sen. was not happy and it was evident from the expression on his face. Before leaving, the Bank's team-manager, Sarma, Sudarsan& Raju were taken to the Brigadier to pay their respects. Mohan was with the Brigadier.

Brig. Prasad was tall, lean and pleasant. Capt. Mohan was strikingly handsome and had a ready smile. From his countenance one can guess that he had a very positive outlook on life. After the Bankmen were introduced, the Brig. asked pleasantly, "How did the match go?"

"It was a draw. The scores were level at 1-1. We did not go for the free kicks as light was fading," replied the Colonel.

"So, the Bank men scored a goal against us"

"In the first half, the Bank team was leading by 1-0. In the second half, they equalized".

"We scored only one goal"

"No Sir. Both the goals were scored by the Bank Team. There was a self-goal by them"

"You know, in some countries like Colombia etc., if you score a self goal, you are a dead man. I am disappointed".

Sarma intervened, "Your team's main objective is combat readiness. The Bank team consists of professionals and each of them represented their states in the Nationals. Assam Rifles was no match to the Bank Team"

"That is a good explanation. Where do you come from?"

"I am from Kona Seema in East Godavari District".

"I am from Vizianagaram," he said in Telugu.

Capt. Mohan said, "I am from Madras, we are Andhras settled in Madras"

Sudarsan was awestruck by the military fitness, discipline and his personal charm. His sister is no match to the Captain. He gave up all hope and lost interest in the alliance.

He asked, "Capt., you never come to the Bank. It is a pleasure to meet you. I would like to meet you more often".

Mohan smiled, "Thank you. I would like it too. Tomorrow is a Sunday. So, you must be free. We can meet tomorrow if you like."

Brig. Prasad said, "Mohan does not waste time. He is a happy man, whatever the situation. Meet him tomorrow and hope that some of his magnetism would rub on to you"

"Will 3 PM at your bank be suitable to you", asked Mohan.

"That would be perfect," said Sudarsan.

Raju addressed the Brigadier and said, "There are very few of us Andhras in your rank".

"They are there. Mostly in Medical, Engineering and Communication"

"Have you seen any action?"

"That is an inappropriate question to ask a Brigadier. Without battle experience, I would not have become a Brigadier. Of course I have been active in the Chinese invasion of 1962; I was in Chamb-Jaurian sectors in 1965, when Pakistan attacked us. They were one kilometre inside our territory. We would have pushed them back, but cease fire was called. I served in the U.N forces at various places to enforce the ceasefire and peace keeping. I climbed Mt. Everest. Is that enough"?

"I am sorry, Sir. That was stupid of me to ask"

"That is alright. I got an opportunity to talk about my battles".

Capt. Mohan said, "The brigadier is a brave warrior. But, he is no match to his wife".

"Mohan don't go into that. I still feel bad about interference in the Military matters"

"Our interest is aroused. You cannot stop now," asked Raju.

"Well, I will explain it myself. I was on duty at the Chinese border in 1962. After the cease fire and restoration of status quo ante, I was transferred to the Chinese border in Ladakh. After two years, I was transferred to the LOC in J&K. After the 1965 war, I was transferred to Ladakh. For four years, I was in war zone. My wife was in Madras looking after the Children and herself. When I was transferred to Ladakh again, she went wild. That night around 9:30 PM, my wife rang up the Chief of Army staff directly to his home number. When he answered, she gave him left and right about my posting. She complained that her husband was targeted and was posted at war zones persistently. His family is denied postings at family stations for a long time. The Chief patiently heard her outbreak and said that he would look into the matter. When I reported at Leh, a military helicopter arrived to pick me up with orders transferring me to Hyderabad. After that I was not touched until now".

"Did the Chief express his reaction to the incident," asked Raju.

"I met the Chief in New Delhi and apologised for her behaviour. The Chief said that he had no hard feelings and that nobody can argue with a woman".

"The life in the services is quite interesting and adventurous. We are also transferred inconveniently but that cannot be compared to your transfers".

The Brigadier complained, "You are using our Imprest account to dump untraceable entries".

Sarma & Sudarsan did not know anything about the matter.

Raju explained, "You must be talking about the credit of Rs 150 which was reversed last week. Due to a clerical error, the amount was credited to your Imprest account. The money should go to 438 ASC supply Co. For three months, nobody complained. It came to light during random checking by the Branch Inspector. Both the military units did not notice it".

The Brig. answered, "We are soldiers, not Accountants".

Raju felt that it was prudent to keep quiet.

The Brig. said, "Well gentleman. It was good to meet you and have interesting conversation. Good bye and Best of luck".

They shook hands and left. At 3 PM sharp next day, the Captain met the three at the Bank. They were talking about the Captain when he arrived.

Sudarsan explained, "The Captain's name and particulars are with my father. They are considering the proposal for marriage alliance for my sister. Now, I feel that the proposal is far beyond my sister's qualification. The Captain can get proposals ten times better than my sister"

Raju said, "Capt. Mohan, can we drop your rank. We will call you Mohan".

"That is exactly what I want"

"Sudarsan's house is very near. We will go there and talk. His mother can cook some snacks for us. We can sit in the garden at the back yard and talk".

"OK. I must leave by 7:30 PM. We have plenty of time".

Sudarsan's father recognized Mohan immediately as he had seen his photograph with his bio-data. When everybody was introduced and sat on the chairs, Sudarsan went into the kitchen to fetch some snacks, His father followed him. Both the parents admonished him for bringing the bride groom without prior intimation. Sudarsan said, "Forget about the proposal. He is too good for Suji. It is a friendly visit and is informal".

While they were talking this and that for an hour, Suji walked in. She had gone to her friend's house. She glanced at all of them with a smile but the glance paused when she saw Mohan and walked away. The maid servant brought some Onion Pakodis and put them on the table. She also placed a jug of water with glasses.

The situation changed dramatically. Sudarsan's father was talking solely to Mohan. His mother brought coffee and served to all of them. She took her place in a chair and started taking interest in Mohan. Suji's friend Seetha came to meet Suji and she took up a chair, Suji also joined them.

Mohan was answering all the questions respectfully and was a hit with the family. After sometime, he got up to leave saying, "I have to be at my place by 7:30. If I am late, my colleagues will get impatient."

He shook hands with everybody including the girls, bowed and touched Sudarsan's parents' feet. The four of them came out and were waiting for the military vehicle to pick up Mohan at the Bank, Mohan spoke to Sarma in low voice after letting the other two go a few steps forward. He said, "It is not normal for us to meet civilians outside the cantonment, especially the strangers. I believe in God and fate. It must have been decided to make me meet you. It was our conversation in Telugu for some time that influenced me to agree to meet you today".

"Yes. We meet Military personnel at work, but never personally, even though the person was a regular visitor and has been known for a long time", said Sarma.

"Exactly. This is a happenstance. In fact, we have a bachelor's meet planned in our mess".

Sarma did not understand the purpose of Mohan's talk and was perplexed by the man's eagerness to say something.

Mohan continued, "I like Sudarsan's family. They are like my own family. I liked his sister at first sight. My family is looking for a suitable girl for me. If they have no objection, I will be very happy to marry her. Don't think that I am sex starved or crazy to suggest marriage with the first girl that I came across. I will give my parents' number. Ask them to get in touch with my family if they are interested. If they are not interested, please let me know."

"I think that they will be interested, they have your bio data and your parent's address".

"Really?. So this meeting is not a happenstance at all. It was pre planned. Am I being taken for a ride? Sudarsan should have informed me"

"It is a mere coincidence. His parents and sister were not aware of us meeting you and Sudarsan's invitation to you is casual. He had no intention of raising the issue of marriage with you. His sister was not at home when we went to the house".

"What did she study?"

"She is doing her post-graduation in Food and Nutrition Technology. She is preparing to write the final exams in a few days".

"That is no hurdle. I have no objection to that".

"As you are frank and forthright, we will settle the matter right away. Let us talk to Sudarsan".

"Don't push things too fast. I have expressed my intention immediately as I may not meet you again. If we part without discussing this issue, I lose an opportunity".

Sarma called, "Sudarsan, stop. We have a few things to discuss".

Raju & Sudarsan stopped. Sarma approached them leaving Mohan behind and said, "You appear to have struck a golden deal. Mohan says he is impressed with your sister and wants to marry her. As both the families are strangers, he requests you to approach his parents".

Sudarsan face glowed with pleasure. He said, "I hope he has not committed a mistake. We will definitely pursue the proposal. My parents and sister should agree. I will try to convince them".

He walked up to Mohan and said, "I am extremely glad to hear that you are interested in my sister. I hope that you are not mistaken. The lady with the green Kanchi silk sari is my mother".

Mohan smiled, "Yes. I realized that"

"The lady who served the snacks to us is our domestic help"

Mohan grinned, "I recognized that too".

"The girl in Punjabi Dress who came in first is my sister. The girl who came later is her friend"

"I like the Punjabi dress"

"Are you sure you want to marry her."

Sarma said, "She is a normal girl. There is nothing to hide. Sudarsan, having grown up with her does not realize that she has grown up to be a beautiful and intelligent woman. There is nothing to hide. Personally I think that you will be very lucky if you marry her. There is nothing negative about her".

Mohan said, "Get in touch with my parents and let me know".

Sudarsan was beaming with pleasure. After seeing Mohan off, the trio went back to Sudarsan's house. His parents were delighted and Suji was so happy with the news she said, "He is extremely handsome and I am lucky, he likes me".

Sudarsan replied, "If I do not love my sister, I would not have brought him to the house. I felt that an informal meeting would be decisive. I may not meet him again if I miss this opportunity. You may approach his family in the normal course. It may take some time and his parents might reject. Now things will move fast, as the boy is on our side".

His sister was really beautiful, educated and is a very good match for Mohan. Sudarsan's mother was slightly worried. She said, "The boy is in Army. There is a risk".

Sujatha said, "More people are dying in accidents, natural calamities, crime and suicides per year than soldiers. Even if I marry an employee or a businessman, I may not be assured of the spouse's longevity and health".

"You are too young to realize the consequences of a war. War is killing the enemy. The threat of premature death is very big".

"India has faced three wars so far. The Chinese war in 1962, the wars with Pakistan in 1965 and for Kashmir after Independence. The death toll in 1962 may have been high because the Army was out numbered, out maneuvered and was ill equipped".

"She is right. Red China became a regional power because of the failure of our leaders", said Sarma.

Raju added, "No General would risk a war if the casualty rate is more than 5%".

"How do you know?" asked the mother.

"I read it in an article in the News Paper".

Sujatha said, "That would be true. A large number of civilians too die in war".

Sudarsan's father said, "Suji appears to have decided to marry him. She is arguing in his favour. It is true that this is a good proposal. It is perhaps true that more people die per year than the soldiers in a war. We have discussed the matter in detail. What do we vote for?"

"I vote in favour," said Suji.

"That is 75% of the voting strength".

"I say, Aye", said Sudarsan.

"OK, I vote in favour too, because she wants it", said Sudarsan's father.

"There is no need for my vote. But I vote in favour", said his mother.

Sarma and Raju did not express their opinion.

Sarma replied to the mother's enquiring look. "We do not matter. We have no locus standi, but we think that they are made for each other". After a few more minutes, they took leave of them and left.

Around 12:30 PM on the following day, Sarma received a phone call from the Brigadier. He asked, "Can I speak to Mr. Sarma".

"Speaking"

"I am Brigadier Prasad. Don't think that I am interfering in a matter which is none of my business. Mohan informed me of the events that have taken place yesterday. There was absolutely no reason for Mohan to meet you. It does not happen without a purpose. Marriages are made in heaven, they say. Please convince her parents that this match is an excellent proposition."

"They are interested, sir. His parents can expect the proposal soon. Let Mohan inform them"

After a few days, Sudarsan's parents visited Mohan's family in Madras.

"My boy has told us to expect you. It appears that an informal and accidental meeting has taken place. Our son is interested, we will visit you in Hyderabad and see the girl. We will ring you up and fix a date", said Mohan's dad.

"You are welcome. Right now, we are living in a rented house. Our own house is under construction in Ashok Nagar. We will pick you up from wherever you are lodged and drop you back".

"We will talk about such arrangement in Hyderabad. Brig. Prasad likes my son and takes a personal interest in him. We may not need conveyance".

"That is OK".

"The Brigadier and his wife also may come with us".

"No problem sir. Two of my son's colleagues will also be present".

A few days later, Sudarsan's dad received a call from Mohan's Dad.

"Tomorrow is Sunday. We wish to come to your house around 4 PM. Please ask your son or his friend to wait for us at the Bank. That will be useful if Mohan cannot remember the route. Wait a minute. Brig. Prasad wants to talk to you".

"Good Morning, sir. I am Brig. Prasad. I am interested in this matter and would like to come too, if you have no objection".

"Not at all sir, your visit will be a privilege"

"Thank You"

Everybody was looking forward to the event. But developments in the neighbouring countries are likely to affect both the families. In East Pakistan, Awami League won the general elections with huge majority. Shaik Mujibur Rehman, the leader of the Awami League went to Pakistan to stake his claim. Negotiations failed and he was arrested. Before being whisked away to prison, he declared Independence of East Pakistan. All India Radio picked up the news and broadcasted it repeatedly to the world. The Pakistan army tried to suppress the rebellion. Bangladesh was born and Mukti Bahini was formed and started to fight for liberation. This was in late 1970. The atrocities committed by the Pakistan Army forced one million people to flee and seek refuge in India. India could not sit idly and watch the developments.

In April 1971, Mohan and company have arrived at Sudarsan's house. As far as they were concerned, the search for a bride was over. After the introductions and refreshments, the bride walked into the room accompanied by her friends. This time, the bride was made up in a simple and attractive saree. Her face was glowing with the facial done by the beauty clinic. Sudarsan realized that his sister is very attractive. She said 'Namaste' to the elders, smiled at Mohan and sat down.

Mohan's mother asked a few questions. She knew that she has no option but to agree to this proposal, but felt that she would have selected the girl any way. She was quite impressed. The girl was pretty and well mannered. The groom's company had decided not to waste time. They told the girl's parents, that they liked their daughter and are willing to proceed further for the marriage.

The girl was asked to leave and Sudarsan's father asked, "What is your expectation, Sir".

"We expect the marriage to be as early as possible", replied Mohan's mother.

"Yes, madam. What do you expect?"

"We already told you. Didn't we".

Sarma intervened, "That is true, madam. He wants to know your requirement".

Mohan's father frowned "What requirements, I have no idea what you want from us".

The Brigadier's wife whispered something in Mohan's mother's ear.

"Ah! You are talking about the dowry. We don't take dowry. The marriage should be arranged by you at your cost. Whatever is to be done by us, will be at our cost. You pay for your part and we pay for our part".

"That is settled then. If the boy wants to talk to the girl, he can do so".

Mohan went to the room and spent about 15 minutes.

Brig. Prasad said, "Perform the marriage as early as possible. The engagement will take place now".

Mohan's mother said, "I have not come prepared for the engagement".

"Well. Make the arrangements now. It is only 4:30 PM. As soon as Mohan comes out, go and buy the necessary things. After the engagement, we shall have dinner and leave".

"I do not have the money now" said Mohan's father.

"Don't worry about that sir. We can arrange the cash", said Sudarsan.

"I don't want your money"

"Take a loan from Sarma and return it tomorrow or at your convenience. We have to find our family Purohit (priest) and make our own purchases".

Sarma said, "Gold is at Rs 15 per gram yesterday. The jewelers and dress material shops will be open. How much will you need".

"I think Rs 5000 will be adequate. Can we take the bride with us for shopping", said Mohan's mother.

"Yes. Her friend will also come with her", said Sudarsan's father.

His mother said, "We should also go for shopping. Will it be alright with you if we order food from a restaurant".

"No problem. But why bring it here. We shall eat out," said the Brig.

"Let us presume that we start at 5:00 PM and meet here again at 7:00 PM" said Sudarsan's Dad.

The Brigadier said, "Before you go any further, I have something to tell you. The turmoil in Pakistan is going to affect us. India cannot sit and watch the atrocities in East Pakistan. There are already seven lakh refugees from East Pakistan and it may cross 10 lakhs soon. India has already recognized Bangladesh as an independent country. Preparations for war with Pakistan are underway. We may have to engage the enemy on both the fronts. If China interferes, there will be few more fronts. Mohan will have to fight at the front. If you want to wait until the war is over, that is up to you".

Mohan had come out from the room and joined them. Sudarsan's parents went inside to speak to their daughter and returned after five minutes.

"My daughter wants to talk to you all", said Sudarsan's father.

"I understand that the Brigadier has broken the Official Secrets Act or its equivalent in the Armed forces. I agreed to marry Mohan, that is how I intend to address him in future, I do not change my decision. Let the proceedings continue. If he is called for duty before the wedding takes place, I will wait for his return. If wedding is over before the war, that is OK with me", said Sujatha.

Sudarsan stared at his sister with awe and admiration, "Marriage halls are fully booked till August"

"Nanna, it will be wedding and war or war and wedding, whichever comes first. He won my heart. If you want me to marry him today, I will do so. Thank you Brigadier for your concern".

The Brigadier said, "Marriage hall is no problem. We can arrange a hall in the cantonment. Marriage can be simple. But, you must arrange a reception after marriage which may be expensive. The drinks and food can be arranged at concessional rates. The cost may be borne by any one of you or shared equally".

"We will pay" said Sudarsan's father.

"We will discuss the details tomorrow. Why involve children in this matter" said Mohan's father.

They left the place on their errands and returned at 7:00 PM. Sarma and the Purohit were waiting. Sudarsan's family also returned from their shopping. The Purohit had confirmed that the horoscopes matched and that the couple would live long with happiness. He conducted the engagement ritual and the ring was slipped on to the finger of the bride. They had dinner at a posh restaurant and dispersed. The Muhurtam for the wedding was fixed at 9:17 PM on May 17. They had more than one month. Mohan was visiting Sujatha whenever he could and talking to her on telephone every day. Nobody in the house answered the telephone when Sujatha was at home. Sujatha had completed her exams for the Post graduate Degree. During the first week of May, The Brigadier called Sudarsan's father and told him that there could be no reception after the wedding. Assam Rifles was deployed at the border with East Pakistan and would be moving on 20th May. He suggested that immediately after the marriage, it should be registered without fail. If it was not done by 19th May, it should wait until normalcy was restored.

The Brigadier warned Sudarsan's family that the military information should not be disclosed to anybody.

The Brigadier said, "We keep it confidential, but the enemy knows somehow" and laughed.

As expected, the marriage had taken place and it was registered. Mohan could not meet Sujatha before leaving, but was calling her whenever possible.

Sudarsan's mother claimed one day, "There will be no war. They are building up the pressure, but it will fizzle out".

"No, Amma. Mohan says war is inevitable. The Army's preparations take time. They have to mobilize troops, prepare a strategy and choose the time. They do not want a third front with China. So, the time is chosen when it will be difficult for China to cross the Himalayas. Yet, troops are deployed near the border with China to face any unforeseen eventuality".

"How can he disclose so much information?

"Amma, no soldier will do that. He is discussing the text book strategies"

There was no war till the end of November. Sarma, Raju and Sudarsan were talking of false alarm. In the first week of December, when Indian Military deployment was so close to the border, that even a child could realize India would attack Pakistan on both the fronts. Pakistan started the war with preemptive air strikes on the Indian Air force bases. India retaliated with the ground, Air and Sea attacks. This was a full scale war. Gloom descended on Sudarsan's family. Suji after all her brave talk, became silent and worried. Sarma and Raju who were involved were also affected by the war. Pakistan was no match to the Indian attack. Indian Navy attacked Karachi and destroyed Pakistani vessels and the port. IAF sorties destroyed the Pakistani air bases and PAF was incapacitated. Indian Navy blocked successfully the bases of Pakistan. The ground forces occupied large chunks of West Pakistan. The war lasted hardly three weeks. The 90,000 strong Pakistani Army in East Bengal surrendered to India as Mitro Bahini (The allied forces) had surrounded Dhaka. That was the shortest and decisive war. Pakistan was beaten thoroughly, humiliated and dismembered. After the Pakistani Army surrendered, India declared ceasefire in the West Pakistan. The war was over within 18 days. Even though India intended to attack, Pakistan drew the first blood.

Mohan called from Dhaka and conveyed his wellbeing. He was proud to have participated in the war. He thanked Brig. Prasad for allowing him to go to the front instead of retaining him at the Battalion Head Quarters.

There was joy and celebration at Sudarsan's house. Suji was glowing with relief and happiness.

THE FAUX PAS

After the liberation of Bangladesh, Raju and Sarma enjoyed carte blanche in Sudarsan's house. They were treated as part of that family. Now that the war was over, Suji is ready to join her husband as soon as he was given a fresh posting. She called the Brigadier and thanked him for all the support given to Mohan.

The Brigadier said, "I did not do him any favour. As a junior commissioned officer, he should be in action and not in Administrative office. He should go through all the operations of the Army. I am not interfering in his postings. If you have a problem with any situations, call me. I will help him. He is very happy. You don't have to wait long".

"Thank you", said Suji, "There will be something positive in every situation. I found him very handsome at first sight. All is well that ends well".

The family moved to their new house two months after the end of the war. Suji had joined her husband and both of them were having great fun and were happy. One evening, Sarma and Raju visited Sudarsan's house. His parents received them gladly. That was their first visit to the new house. Sudarsan's father had taken them on a tour of the house. The house was four feet above the road. Sudarsan's father had taken them to the drawing room and then the living room which was 'L' shaped. After length of the living room, it turned right to accommodate the dining room. The kitchen was accessible through the dining room. It was located on the South east of the house. There was Pooja (prayer) Room on the left of the dining room which was on the north east side of the house. There were three bedrooms on the south of the living room. Due to the third bedroom, which protruded beyond drawing room, there was a 11' x 11' verandah. The group entered the master bedroom, where the parents slept. There was the toilet opening into an enclosure of 8' x 8'. Two bedrooms open into the square and entrance to the toilet was through this opening. The toilet was spacious. Sarma and Raju appreciated the tasteful construction.

They went into the third bedroom which was also spacious. A separate toilet was attached to that bed room.

"This is Sudarsan's bedroom. This is the toilet", said his father and opened it. Sudarsan was inside, taking shower. He screamed as soon as the door opened. Startled, his father too screamed and shut the door. Raju and Sarma had a full view of Sudarsan. Raju had seen him earlier during the medical examination.

Sudarsan's father was gasping for breath.

"He almost gave me a cardiac arrest. Why should he scream so loudly. When he is expecting guests, he should take the shower before they arrive or he should lock the door".

Sarma said, "Sudarsan is shy. He protested at the time of Medical examination, when Doctor asked him to take off his clothes".

"But that was two years ago. I am his father and you two are his best friends".

"He is grown up now. Even the parents should respect his modesty".

Raju intervened, "We cannot blame Sudarsan. This is his bedroom and his toilet. We got only a glimpse of his head. We guessed that he was taking a shower as his head was covered with shampoo. We should have knocked before opening the door".

"You did not see him?"

"No. You blocked the view. The house is beautiful and tastefully decorated and furnished. Congratulations", Sarma commented, "The house is airy and well lit".

"Thank you. Let us go to the drawing room", said Sudarsan's father. He told himself inaudibly, "Lucky, his sister or his mother were not in the shower".

Sudarsan came out and joined them. His father said, "Now that Suji is married, we will search for a suitable bride for Sudarsan".

Sudarsan said, "I will not come to meet the brides more than once. I don't want to go to the bride and hurt her by declining. You screen all the proposals and select the one that suits me. The photographs give us a general idea but the girl may not look as good as she is in the photo. If you like a match, you see the girl and the family, only after you are fully satisfied, I will come".

"The bride's parents may not like to show the girl if the groom is not coming".

"Whatever is to be done, I do not wish to come to see the bride more than once or twice".

"Suji is lucky to have met Mohan informally. I am also looking for such an opportunity".

After this discussion, all the three of them left the house and dispersed.

Leela approached Raju while he was at work and reported, "Satyanarayana from Premises and Estate department came to me and talked to me for nearly half an hour. He was trying to make friends. I am compelled to engage in conversations with people who are interested in me. I am not able to concentrate on my work.

Raju said, "That problem will be solved if you marry. Even after the marriage, some wolves will be after you to seduce you".

"How should I cope up with the problem"

"You should be tactful and firm in dealing with such people. You may at some time have an extra marital affair after several years of marriage. You may be bored with your husband. The same man in bed year after year may motivate you to have an affair"

"You think that extra marital sex is wrong"

"I am not teaching you the morals. Such affair may lead to problems not anticipated. All religions say that is a sin. Personally I think that it is a pleasant sin".

"All sins are pleasant. Otherwise the heaven will be over crowded. I don't think that I will be interested in such affairs".

"I am interested, but I don't want to get involved in serious trouble. I know of such instances in other organisations. One husband committed suicide, another abandoned the family and was not seen again. The wife needed to be supported by the lover. He hates it but had no choice".

"In the bank, two or three of the ladies have affairs and appear to be enjoying thoroughly. Surayah says it is not worth the trouble. Barring the three or four women, others in the Bank are having excellent time, with their spouses. The other man may be no different from the husband, which is most likely. There is no tension, fear of the family learning of the illegitimate relationship etc. Surayah further says after enjoying sex, men normally lose interest and some may, you do not know what you are getting into, try to take advantage by blackmail".

"I am surprised that Surayah advised you against such things. She believes that everybody, repeat everybody will commit adultery. They stay loyal to the family until an opportunity comes. I think that Surayah is right. Such situations may lead to crime and murder out of jealousy. Surayah tells me differently. She says that I am wasting opportunities".

"Somebody is waiting at my desk. We will continue the discussion later", said Leela and went back to her desk.

Raju was not happy. There is nagging feeling of something amiss. This had been present since the day of joining the Bank. He did not mention it to anybody as he did not know what it was.

After lunch, Raju approached Leela and said, "You better take a decision on marriage. You are too good looking to procrastinate it. You will continue to be bothered by the aspirants".

Leela replied, "I am tired of people telling me that I am beautiful. I may not have competition in the Bank, but in the glamour world of fashion and movies. I am just one of them, may be at the bottom in the rankings. I prefer the job I am doing. I will marry a man I like and my family approves. What happened to the man making threatening calls. He did not call again".

"Didn't we tell you? When we met him and discussed the matter, he was ashamed and promised not to bother. Are you interested in him?"

"No, no, not at all. I just wondered what he was up to".

"There was misunderstanding. He is well educated, rich and intelligent and a sportsman. It is not his character to make such calls. He was trying to get a date from you so that he can explain his feelings to you".

"What sport was he interested in?"

"He is a Boxer. He has been boxing since his school days. He continued it even in U.S when he was studying MBA. He is not a champion, but a regular Boxer. His priority was education. He has to take over his father's industries when the time comes. He is very good looking, well-built and very polished in his behaviour. If you are interested, we can arrange a meeting".

"No. I am not interested. People mistake infatuation to love. Besides, he is a complete stranger. I am told that you practice the martial arts and hold some belt".

"Yes. I believe that a martial art should be learned compulsorily".

"The anonymous caller must be a member of the Boxing Association. With his kind of riches, he can be very easily made a member. Boxing championship tournament is underway in Hyderabad. I am not interested in that sport. He is a complete stranger. I cannot accept him".

The dialogue ended and Raju returned to his seat.

At 5:30 PM the group of five were sitting at Sarma's seat. Vivek approached them and said, "There are boxing championships going on in LB stadium. I reached the quarter final. In the quarter final, I am fighting a Manipuri Boxer from the Services tomorrow. My bout is at 4:30 PM. Tomorrow is Saturday. Will you be interested in watching it and encouraging me".

"Definitely", said Sarma.

"Do you know Ravi Sankar?" asked Raju.

"He is a big shot and wields considerable clout in the Association. He is a Boxer too and a good one. Do you know him", asked Vivek.

"I met him only once. We will come tomorrow and sit as close to the ring as possible".

At 4:00 PM the five of them reached the stadium and were looking for a place near the ring. They saw Ravi Sankar near the ring. He was talking to one of the judges. He glanced at the group, recognized Sarma and Raju and smiled. After concluding his briefing with the judge, he came to them and asked, "I did not know that you were interested in Boxing. I have never seen you at the Boxing clubs".

"No, we are not interested. We have come to cheer our colleague Vivek fighting the quarter final".

"Vivek? I know him. He is a promising boxer. He is only Twenty one. He has the potential to win an international title. I will arrange seats for you near the ring".

They were given the seats in the second row behind the Judges. Ravi Sankar explained that, "Each bout has three rounds. Each round is of three minutes duration. There is a short time-out between each round. I think Vivek has a fair chance as he is tall and has longer reach. Points are given for each punch that landed on the opposition. Abdomen punches do not earn points unless the opponent buckles or falls. If the opponent falls and does not get up by the count of ten it is a Knock Out. Have a nice time, I will send you some snacks and tea. Don't look for me to say good bye. I am busy."

The five watched the match between a boxer from Haryana and the opponent is from U.P. In Haryana, boxing is popular. The Haryana Boxer was so superior that by the end of the second round, his score was 22 while the opponent scored three. During the match, Sarma and Syam were screaming, "Stop the fight. Referee, stop the fight", in the first round itself. The referee stopped the fight after the second round. The Haryana Boxer qualified for the semifinal.

The next quarter final match was between Vivek and a Manipuri. As soon as the Boxers took position at their corner, Sarma & company have started chanting loudly Vivek's name. Other spectators caught the act and chanted loudly the name of their favourite boxer. The referee and the judges looked at this group as soon as they started chanting. They were waving to the crowd to remain silent as the match was about to start.

The bell rang. Vivek had the advantage of height and the reach of his hands. The Manipuri, Moirangtum, was shorter and as a result shorter reach. But he was defensive. He spent most of the time stalling. When Vivek lost his patience, he was moving forward and landing a punch. Before he could pull back the hand, the Manipuri was scoring a point as Vivek's guard was open. At the end of the first round, the score was 3-2 in favour of Vivek. Second round was no different and Vivek was behind with 2-3. In the third round, the score was 3-3. During the last minute, Vivek scored one point. The last fraction of the second the Manipuri scored a point and within a blink Vivek scored a point. The bell rang. Vivek qualified for semi-finals.

There were several weight categories which none of the bankers remembered. The semi-final involving Vivek was scheduled for on Wednesday. So, none of them could attend. As Vivek was not appointed on the Sports quota, he applied for the leave on Wednesday. The semifinal was at 3:30 PM. Around 6:30PM, Vivek came to Sarma's table when he was about to close his desk and was preparing to leave. As usual, the five were to proceed to the Irani Hotel, chat for a few minutes over tea. That day, Vivek joined them. They did not realise at that time that the group of five would become a group of six.

The final match was on the Sunday again at 3:30 PM. Vivek was to fight with the Haryana boxer who reached the finals in his group beating a Bihari Boxer.They entered the stadium early and took seats close to the ring. They came prepared with the junk food to while away the time. They could not eat during a bout. Ravi Sankar was passing by, looked at them, smiled and asked them by gestures if they needed anything. He noticed that they found good seats and walked away.

The Haryana Boxer was an equal match to Vivek. Both of them were of the same height and weight. The Boxers took up their places in diagonally opposite corners. The referee called them to the centre. The rivals nodded at each other in acknowledgement. The bell rang. Both the Boxers were stalking each other looking for an opening. They were stalling for most of first minute. Both became impatient, moved closer and started throwing punches and defending themselves. Haryana Boxer scored the first point in the second round. First round, the score was 0-0. Vivek had earlier told them that the Haryana Boxer was superior by training and practice. At the end of the second round, the score was 5-2 in favour of Haryana. Vivek and his coach had drawn up a strategy to overcome the Haryana Boxer's superiority, but it was not working. During the time out after the second round, the coach was loudly advising Vivek.

"You are giving him a lot of openings and he is clever enough to seize the opportunity. In this round, he will try to keep his distance from you as he is already ahead of you. You have to chase him and beat him. Use combinations. With this kind of opponent, you are not likely to get an opportunity for combinations. You must deceive him. Feign a right but punch straight. If that doesn't connect, immediately follow up with a hook. Improvise the technique. You should think on your feet. Do your best. The coach was speaking so loudly in Telugu that it was loud and clear on the loud speakers and the T.V. But, the Haryana corner could not understand a word of it.

The bell rang for the third round. The Boxers had come to the centre of the ring and were stalking each other. As anticipated, the Haryana Boxer was stalling around Vivek in the ring. Vivek chased him down and landed clean and clear punches and scored three points in succession. The score was equal at 5-5. The opponent was now desperate for clean and straight punches. He was coming forward to connect to Vivek. Vivek could not try the combinations as the opponent was very fast. During the last 50 seconds of the final round of the bout, both came forward with open faces in a desperate attempt to lead. As there was an opening, both of them punched with all their power. Both connected simultaneously. Vivek received the punch with great force on his right cheek bone. Colours of light flashed in his head. Without realizing, he staggered blindly on his feet and has taken two seconds to return to normal. The flashing colours vanished leaving a blank whiteness like T.V. screen gone blank. The whiteness was replaced by the referee's face watching his face closely so that he could stop the fight, if he didn't regain normalcy.

Everybody in the stadium was watching Vivek's discomfort. When Vivek started jumping, the eyes turned to the Haryana Boxer. He was sitting on one leg folded at the knee, the other leg upright, folded at knee. He was covering his eye with his hand. He received a punch with great force just below the left eyebrow. There was a cut. His left eye was blinded by the blood dripping from the cut. The fight was over with twenty seconds to spare. It was a knock out. Vivek won the Gold and qualified for the forthcoming Asian Games. The five Bankers and the officials at the Vivek's corner were jumping and shouting with joy.

Vivek met Ravi Shankar a few days later. Ravi Shankar congratulated Vivek and assured him of any support he needed.

Sudarsan's father came to the Bank one day on business. He greeted Sarma and sat on the chair opposite, while his transaction was being processed. He told Sarma, "I went to a Kerala Ayurvedic hospital as you suggested. They prescribed some medicines and a massage for eight days. The massage was uncomfortable. They asked me to take off my clothes including the underwear. They gave me a flimsy Khadi piece of cloth to cover my private parts. The back was not covered. They poured some hot oil into my navel and started massage. There were two guys, one for each side. Strangely when the hot oil was poured, I felt a chill. After rubbing the oil on my body starting with the foot to neck in one sweep for about half an hour, they asked me to turn back up. The same process was repeated. Starting with the underside of the foot, they massaged my back. So far, so good. If you sign in for a massage, you cannot refuse to take the clothes off. But after each sweep, they were squeezing my butts followed by loud pat. I did not understand what it was for. I felt violated. They were more like slaps. The masseur on the left was scoring more pats than the right one. I did not make any comments. I finished the course and took their medicines for two weeks as prescribed and it was finally over".

"How do you feel now"

"There is a lot of improvement. That school of medicine works".

"Well, that is a relief".

"Sudarsan is giving as trouble. He does not want to see the brides to be. He leaves everything to us. After we screen all the proposals and select one girl, he would come to see the girl. The bride's side is reluctant to show the girl if the boy doesn't come".

"He doesn't want to see a girl and decline to marry her and hurt her feelings. If we are satisfied in all aspects, he will visit the family and take a decision".

"We have no choice but to comply with his stipulation".

"How is Suji? Is she happy?"

"They are both extremely happy and are thoroughly enjoying their lives. We are happy too as things have gone very well", saying this he got up to leave. He said, "When we go to see a girl, will you and Raju come with us. You are both part of our family. The bride's side will have to find two more chairs and two more cups of coffee".

"Definitely, but see to it that the arrangement is fixed on a Saturday or Sunday. Raju can come on other days, but I cannot leave my work half done. I cannot entrust it to others half way through, because everybody will be busy and there is the matter of accountability. I may have to take leave".

"Noted," said he and left.

Leela approached Raju and said, "What is cooking today?"

"Same as any other day. One day is no different from the previous day"

"O.K. I am leaving for home. Good night".

"Wait a minute. I have something to tell you. You remember your complaint about the threatening calls. We met him again few days back. You misunderstood him. He was trying to get an opportunity to talk to you. He didn't say so to us, but that is what we understood. It is not his character to threaten you. He is very well educated, rich and a sportsman. He is very decent. He must have mistaken infatuation for love. He does not appear to be interested any more. He can find his bride. If you want to consider him, we can arrange a meeting at your house. I hope that he will reconsider the situation".

Leela replied, "That is a closed chapter. I am not interested in riches and his influence. I want a man who will keep me happy and will take good care of me. I think that is what everybody wants. But, after marriage, we have to eat and have an address. He should have a decent job"

"I hope you will get the husband you want. You are too beautiful and gifted to marry an ordinary guy. Good night".

In the evening, the five of them were sitting in the Irani restaurant and were chatting. They were joined by Vivek. The five have become six now, as Vivek is joining them whenever possible. The Bank converted Vivek into sports category and he had more time to practice.

Sarma said, "Sudarsan's father is complaining that Sudarsan is not cooperating in the search for a suitable bride".

"Why should I visit all those girls I am not likely to marry and so on. I feel bad about saying that I do not want that alliance".

"But you are leaving the burden to your parents".

"Yes. In the arranged marriages, you can only look at the brides for a few minutes. Now a days, they are allowing the boy and girl to talk to each other. The family back ground, compatibility etc. are taken care of by the parents. All men and women do not have an opportunity to find their perfect soul mates and remain unmarried for a long time. Boyfriends and girlfriends do not become spouses and break up in many cases. I prefer an arranged marriage".

Vivek interfered and said, "Ravi Sankar told me at first sight he fell for Leela. He tried to meet her outside the Bank, but that did not materialize. He realised that he could forget about her and stay normal. He was not affected by her after a few days and could easily carry on his day to day activities without thinking of her. I thought that Leela missed a good bride groom, but now, I think she was wise to decline to meet him as he could forget about her so easily".

"With so many new recruits, most of our conversations are only about girls, marriages etc. We should talk about other things too, such as inflation, the wars with our neighbours, Pakistan and China and a million other subjects", complained Sarma.

Two months later, Sudarsan's father came to the Bank and informed Sarma, "We finally zeroed in on a suitable girl for Sudarsan. Can we arrange the visit for the coming Sunday about 4:30 P.M."

"That will be fine with us. Raju and I shall be at your house by 3 P.M. Sudarsan did not tell us about this?"

"He does not know yet. We will discuss this alliance tonight".

Raju and Sarma were at Sudarsan's home promptly at 3 P.M on Sunday. Sudarsan was dressed casually. Sarma and Raju did not like his clothes. Raju said, "Sudarsan, I hope you are not going to come wearing these clothes. They look shabby".

"I intend this to be an informal affair. I am comfortable with them".

Sarma said, "You should wear good clothes, look your best for this occasion. Also, be prepared with some topics/subjects to talk to her".

Raju said, "Don't be too confident about this match. Just as you have the right to say 'No', the girl also has the same right. If there are no fresh clothes, we will buy them. Have a shave and shower and makeup your face. We will get you a pair of new shirts and trousers. There is time".

Sudarsan was worried now. If she declined, he will be hurt and take a long time to overcome the feeling. He remembered the incident with the Doctor during the Medical Examinations. Sudarsan's father said, "Well said. After all, he is only a clerk in the Bank. There are job security and career opportunities. The girls have their own requirements. You cannot take things for granted".

Raju said, "I feel that he better wear new clothes. Give me a trouser and shirt you are comfortable with. I will bring pair of new clothes".

Sarma said, "I will come with you. We can be back in half an hour".

Sudarsan's father said, "While you are at it, will you bring some flowers, fruits and sweets for the girl".

"O.K. sir", said Sarma.

They returned after 40 minutes. Sudarsan was looking fresh and handsome. But, his worry had become tension as he realized that the girl also has the choice.

Sudarsan gratefully accepted the new clothes. After Sudarsan was dressed up to the satisfaction of everybody, they left for the house of the bride to be. They arrived at 4:30 P.M. There was no need to introduce the bride-groom, as he was dressed for the occasion. Sudarsan's father introduced his son, Sarma and Raju and all of them were seated. Raju and Sarma have taken the chairs at the end of row and Sudarsan was seated on the first single sofa, opposite him was a vacant chair for the girl.

After a few minutes of discussions about the relatives and friends of each family, refreshments were served. A few minutes later the girl walked in, took up position on the vacant chair opposite that of Sudarsan. The girl was properly dressed and made up for the occasion. Sudarsan was quite impressed by her looks. He quietly whispered in his mother's ear, "I hope she doesn't say no to me".

His mother whispered back, "Don't worry. You look great. Be confident".

After the questions and answers session, the girl's father pointed to a room and said, "Both of you can talk to each other now in that room".

Sudarsan stood up and his trouser fell to floor. Everybody was stunned by the mishap. The girl was bent forward with her face covered by both hands and the face on her knees. She was convulsing silently with uncontrollable laughter. Sudarsan was standing red faced, with shame.

The girl's father said, "That will not be necessary, sir. We are not such indecent family to scrutinise the private parts. We look at the personality, job and family back ground. Please pull up your trousers".

Her father's comments made the situation worse for the girl. He did not realise that it was an accident and not a wilful show off.

The girl could not contain herself and broke into loud and uncontrollable peals of laughter.

Sudarsan pulled up his trousers and said, "The situation is goofed up. She will not marry me now. Let us go".

The girl still unable to contain her peals somehow managed to say, "I will". She finally controlled herself and said, "As you were interested in me and almost said so, I will marry you, but not now. Let the marriage take place in regular manner with all the celebrations".

The girl's father said, "Please forgive my daughter for laughing at your son's embarrassment. We realised that your son expressed his willingness to marry my daughter. With the trousers down, my daughter also agreed for this alliance, we can discuss other matters. Let the boy and girl go to the room and talk to each other.

As the bride-groom and bride exited, the girl's father asked, "What is your expectation, Sir".

"I asked the same question at the time of my daughter's marriage. Now, I thoroughly understand your question. We do not want any dowry. Whatever arrangements we should make, will be made at our cost, you take care of your side of the cost of the wedding".

"Thank you, Sir. We will meet you during this week to fix up a date and Muhurtam etc. We are proud of your alliance, Thank you".

LEFT, RIGHT AND STRAIGHT

Sarma, Raju and Syam met at the usual rendezvous at the gate of the Osmania University road at 5:30 A.M. The road was blocked by the Police to prevent vehicles on that road. The barricades will be removed at 7 A.M. and vehicular traffic allowed. The road is clean with a number of trees lined up along the length of the road. There are beautiful lawns spread in front of University buildings. Some of the lawns are occupied by the yoga teachers and learners. They will also vacate the lawns before the barricades are removed. People could be seen walking brusquely and jogging according to their abilities.

Sarma said, "This is a beautiful and perfect place with fresh air. This is the least polluted area for early morning exercises".

Raju said, "There are several places in Hyderabad extremely suitable for morning exercises. There is Tank Bund, where traffic is not allowed till 7 A.M. But the water is polluted and stinks. There is Jalagam Vengala Rao Park in Road No.1 of Banjara Hills, KBR Park in Jubilee Hills, Indira Gandhi Park in Domalaguda and several other places. But, the wonders of Hyderabad and surroundings are the boulders. The hills are not single block like mountains of the Eastern Ghats. The boulders appear to be placed precariously by nature".

Syam intervened, "We are here to jog and not for chatting. Let's start".

They started jogging from the Andhra Mahila Sabha College till the end of the road beyond the Police Station and return. If anyone was tired, he was dropping back. Raju took 30 minutes to complete, Syam 45 minutes and Sarma longer than both of them. After completing this ritual, they sit on a lawn and rest. After the normal breath is restored, they chat for some time and disperse.

Syam said, "Now, let us talk about the boulders. They are wonderful. I don't know how they evolved".

Sarma replied, "Millions of years ago an earthquake of very high intensity must have occurred breaking the mountains in to piles of boulders. That is only a guess".

Raju said, "More than a million years ago, the sea was up to Suryapet. From Suryapet to the coast, only fish fossils are found. The earth quake Sarma talked about must have lifted the ground and created the Deccan Plateau. This is also a surmise. These boulders must have formed during the earth quake. The mountain must have broken up into boulders".

"That sounds reasonable, but the surmises are not substantiated by scientists. May be they are confirmed. I do not know much about science".

Sarma, "Hyderabad is above the sea level and the Andhra coast is almost at the sea level. That is why all the rivers in the state flow east. Machilipatnam is one metre below the sea level".

"This is the kind of conversation we should have. We are always talking about girls and marriages", said Sarma.

"What is wrong with talking about girls. You are hardly 30 years old. Of course, you are married, but you may not be disinterested in girls", complained Syam.

"Let's go. We will be late for work", said Raju.

In the evening, when they were all sitting together, Syam complained, "The early morning exercises are making me tired. I am dozing off during work".

"In that case stop jogging. Practice yoga at home. You have the problem of the torso that is developed unequally. You will become regular soon. But train from a guru. Otherwise you may hurt yourself", advised Raju.

"I will have to get up at 5 A.M. to attend the classes. That doesn't solve my problem".

"Walking is recommended as good and simple form of staying fit. But, I think it controls cholesterol and nothing more. Jogging, I feel is slightly better because your legs will become strong and you will lose fat. Yoga is better. All three of them make you feel fresh once you are accustomed to them".

"Yoga is a fundamental principle. Martial Arts, Bharata Natyam are dynamic forms of it. People may scream that it is absurd. Most of the stances in the martial arts are yogic. Yoga is static and the others the dynamic forms of yoga. Additional benefits of yoga are Pranayaam, meditations, concentration and spiritualism. It does not propagate any religion. I think that I will take up yoga. This jogging is wearing me out", said Sarma.

Leela and two other girls were passing by Sarma's table on their way home after work. Leela asked jovially, "What are you guys plotting. You look sinister".

"We are plotting the overthrow of the Shah of Iran", said Chakri.

"What are you guys doing with this gay person. All of you are married".

"I am not gay. I like girls", said Raju.

"Why don't you get married. Haven't found the perfect girl yet? I wonder if you can recognize your soul mate when you see her. What kind of girl do you want".

"Firstly, I don't want a working woman. I want a full time house wife".

"You are still in early decades of the Twentieth Century. You are either a jealous man or obsolete. Wait for a few more years and you become too old to be interesting to any proposal. I can help you. I know a lady who meets your requirement".

"Who is she?" asked Sarma.

"She is the mother-in-law of my class mate. Her husband died a few years ago". Everybody grinned. They realised that she was making fun of Raju.

"How old is she?", asked Chakri.

"She must be close to sixty. I don't know if she will be willing to marry again. If Raju asked me, I will follow up the matter".

"Can she bear children", asked Syam grinning.

"I don't know. He has got to try. There is nothing wrong in trying. She had hysterectomy long ago. But miracles happen. He should try hard. He also saves the wages of the cook, house keeper etc. He can try. As Gita says, 'you have the right to action, but not to the fruits there of' Best of Luck, Raju. Good night everybody".

They all enjoyed the conversation and were all smiling. Raju commented, "The trouble with her is that she is beautiful and knows it. She is arrogant".

Sarma said, "Why don't you ask her to marry you".

Raju replied, "She is in denial mode. She has declined excellent proposals. I am not worthy of her. My parents are searching for a suitable bride. If she says no to me, I may lose interest in marriage".

"I think it is better to get it over with. What has been bothering you is perhaps the suspense about her attitude towards you. Propose and get a 'no' for an answer. I think you will recover in a couple of months and be normal".

"May be you are right. I will do something about it".

After a couple of days, Raju was passing by Leela's desk and smiled at her. She smiled back. Raju asked, "I observed that the middle aged lady sitting with you for process of her transaction was talking to you very pleasantly".

"Yes. She was saying that I am very special and whoever marries me will be a very lucky man".

"She is right"

"There is nothing special about me. I only have wide, dark brown eyes, long dark brown hair, oval face with a dimple on the right cheek, a perfect nose, very attractive mouth, without the curled up lips. I am tall and slim".

"You never give others an opportunity to point out your special features".

"No. They look at me as a whole and do not observe my features. I am proud of my hair which is long and falls to the floor when I sit in my chair. It takes a lot of time to dry. I apply coconut oil and after sometime wash it with shampoo. I like to wear my hair clean and dry. I sit with the blower and practice carnatic music for one hour".

"I agree with everybody. You are really beautiful", said Raju moving on.

Raju told Sarma, "Ravi Sankar is the worthy match for her. Both of them are not interested".

"Marriages are made in heaven. I believe it. She is intelligent and knows what she wants. You have not yet decided?"

"That nagging feeling that something amiss may not be due to Leela. Let me understand myself first. Both Geeta and Bible say, 'Know thy self'. I am trying to do that'".

"Best of luck. Do it fast. Don't take a lot of time. Her parents must be looking for a suitable boy".

"I will. Beauty is not always a gift. It could trigger dejected suitors to go for extreme actions like throwing acid and injure her physically or pester her for one opportunity. She is handling people well. I see only plus points. There is nothing negative about her".

Vivek joined the group that evening. As the Bank has decided to treat him as a sports category employee, he is allotted to dispatch section. He is free to leave after lunch. For any sports related events, he need not apply for leave. There are other benefits too. Syam asked, "You do exercises with weight and other equipment. How do you manage to develop both sides equally".

"I heard of your problem. You can get it corrected in a gym. The coach there will give you suitable advice and equipment".

"Syam, why do you need six packs? People can see them only if you take off your shirt. Vivek's case is different. It is necessary for him to have rippling muscles in his sport" remarked Sarma.

"Boxing is a contact sport and can cause permanent injury", said Chakri.

"That is misconception. Great care is taken to avoid injury to the Boxers. Injury is possible in Cricket, Football, and Hockey etc. Boxing appears to be more hazardous. There is no need to worry about blood and incapacitations. It is a reasonably safe sport".

Raju said, "Everybody should train to fight. That should be compulsory. Nonviolence can be practiced only by the one who is capable of violence. If you do not know how to fight, you don't have to practice Ahimsa. You are non violent by incompetence".

"Syam, join Vivek in his gym. There, you can consult the coach. I am quite sure that the muscles will become normal if you wait for some time", said Sarma.

"How did your wife feel about the muscles", asked Chakri.

Sarma interfered and said, "That is an intimate matter of his family. If he doesn't volunteer, you should not ask. Don't reply Syam".

There was a suggestion of a movie, but only Raju and Vivek accepted. They called it a day and left leaving Raju and Vivek to go to a movie.

Next day Raju told Sarma, "I have decided to take your advice and settle the matter with Leela at an opportune moment".

A few days later, at the close of office hours, Raju approached Leela and asked her, "Today everybody in our group has important affairs to attend to. They left for their homes. I am alone and do not know what to do with the evening. I am planning to go to a movie. Will you come with me".

"I am free too. Which picture shall we see. Have you selected the movie".

Raju was speechless. Leela has accepted the date proposed by him.

She looked up as there was no response from Raju.

She said, "Have I fired a stun gun at you? Why are you looking like a stricken man? Please close your mouth. It is wide open and I can see that you have healthy teeth. Why should we go to a movie? We cannot talk.

Let us go to a restaurant and spend some time. I don't want to come to an ordinary restaurant. I am a five star date. Find a five star hotel".

Raju was still dumb founded.

Leela looked at him and asked, "You have no money. Is it not?"

Raju said, "It is true that I have no money. But I can get the cash within half-an-hour".

"You will borrow from Sarma or others. You will explain to them the situation. I don't like it".

Raju was silent guiltily.

"This is the first date of my life and you don't have any money".

"I thought you would say no"

"If you thought I would decline, why did you invite me? The more and more I speak to you the more and more I regret the decision taken by me".

Raju still didn't have anything to say.

"O.K. I will pay the bills, but it should be returned to me tomorrow. The interest rate is 100% per day".

Raju said, "Thank you. I have the money in my account. I will repay the amount tomorrow with interest".

They went to a five star hotel in Banjara Hills. She lost her foul mood and was talking pleasantly. Raju said, "People tell me that your mother still looks like your sister. She is also beautiful".

"My mother married when she was going on nineteen. I was born to her when she was twenty one. She is only 43 years old. As you said, she is very good looking".

How about your dad? Is he hand-some".

"Yes. Very. He doesn't come to the Bank. All the excellent features of mine described by me are actually the words said to me by people courting me. I am tired of people telling me that I am beautiful. You don't go to a girl and propose marriage if you think she is ugly. I may be attractive but will be plain in the company of the models and film stars. Besides, I can't stand the public glare".

"I think you are very pretty. Thank you for accepting my invitation. You never dated anybody so far".

"Even though we are not dating, we have been talking to each other for the last two years and know each other. I don't date anybody. He has got to be someone special".

"Thank you"

"Don't assume too much in this meeting. I can't keep on declining and make people believe that I am inaccessible. I like men. I enjoy their flattery. By dating several people, I may get the reputation of loose character"

"Thanks again for choosing me"

"That is alright. My parents are worried too. I am the only child to them. They don't want to commit a mistake they would regret for the rest of their lives. But, they would accept the man I choose unless it is a bad choice. I do not wish to defy them".

Raju picked up enough courage to say, "I love you. I know that I am not your league. But I don't think I will be happy with anybody else. My parents are looking for suitable girl for me. I cannot postpone marriage proposals indefinitely. Will you marry me?"

Leela's face went red.

She said, "You flirt with every woman. I will go a little further and say that you flirt with any female whether a woman or a cat or a dog or a cow. You flirt unnecessarily without any commitment. You raise the girl's hopes and don't follow up. Some of the girls are angry and really mad at you".

"I don't want any trouble"

"Do you think that the girls want trouble? You lack the seriousness and intent but still flirt with them. Imagine the girl's situation"

"I am sorry now about my behaviour. I thought I was being friendly"

"How do you expect me to take your proposal seriously".

Raju was on the point of weeping. She was courteous and reasonable with suitors she declined. But, in his case she was expressing disgust and was insulting. He had no answer to her comments. Leela continued, "You and your group of friends talk of nothing but sex and girls. I wonder how Sarma is coping up with you?"

"You have delivered a hook that connected to my right cheek bone and it hurts. I am sorry for what I have done and apologise to the girls".

"That is the stupidest thing to do. It appears that the left hook is not enough. Now try to block or duck the right".

"Is there something more?"

"Yes, you have no purpose in life. You have landed in this Bank job. You think that life will go on smoothly and there is nothing more to do".

"I have hobbies. I read voraciously and practice martial arts".

"When do you do that. You come to Bank at 9 AM and spend time with Sarma and leave late in the evening along with your friends. What do you read".

"Anything. Fiction, History, Economics, Mathematics and so on. I read every book I come across, whatever the subject".

"How do you find time for all these things. You spend most of the free time in the Bank"

"I don't come early every day. Evenings we break up early. Syam is married, Chakri and Sudarsan are engaged to be married. They leave early to spend time with their fiance's. Even otherwise, I read till late in the night".

"You are bluffing. You are a sex starved psycho who doesn't care about people who come in contact with you, but pretend interest and friendship. You are a humbug".

"Enough. Your right hook too connected. I know that I am not worthy of you. But, if I do not ask you, I will regret it for the rest of my life. I am not a sissy to shed tears or weep silently, but I am disappointed. In a couple of days, I will recover from this disgrace. Thank you for the frank opinion. I am really grateful. Please pay the bill and let us leave"

"It is not over yet, you have to take the straight before we finish this conversation"

"I hope the straight doesn't connect. Fire away"

"Despite all the defects in your personality and character, you had the temerity to ask for my hand. Now take this straight. I love you too. Yes. I will marry you. When I first saw you, I knew that I found my man. You enjoy a good reputation with the girls. I have been declining all proposals for marriage from the suitors or grooms to be selected by my family. I told my parents about you. They said that they would give their opinion after talking to you".

"The straight punch connected so hard that I am knocked out. This is the happiest knock out, not likely to be enjoyed by anybody else".

"You took your sweet time, didn't you. I almost gave up. I believed that you were gay".

"I am not gay. I like women. I am a one woman man"

"You better be"

Raju was beaming with happiness. He was sure that his life with this girl would be happy and exciting without a moment's boredom.

Leela said, "Let us finish eating. I want you to meet my parents. We need their consent. They are waiting".

"How did you know that I will be proposing to you. I did not know it myself. You did not use the telephone since I asked you to spend the evening with me"

"There is a formula, dude. There is a formula"

"What is the formula? That would be useful to many girls"

"If the formula is known to everybody, men will become immune to it".

In fact, she asked her friends in the Bank to inform her parents.

"In the West, the boy and girl kiss each other to cement the proposal".

"We are not in the West. We are in India, Kissing in public is not tolerated. You have to wait till the marriage is over".

"Well, I am so happy that I have to kiss or I will go crazy".

"If you insist, kiss the waiter. In the West, they slip a diamond ring on the girl's finger. You don't have the ring nor the money"

"I can get the ring in half an hour"

"I have a confession to make. Ravi Sankar did not threaten me. He was very polished and courteous. But there is no way I can marry him. His riches and personality did not impress me. He was a complete stranger. Wealth may not bring happiness. No doubt, one should have enough to eat and have a house to live. Besides, I have made up my mind already. When you met him, he realised that I have decided on you. That is why he did not call again".

Raju laughed aloud. Leela asked him to explain his laughter. That was their 40th marriage anniversary. "I remembered our first date. You delivered a speech that is impossible to forget. I was on the point of shedding tears until you delivered the straight. I am lucky to have married you."

"You deserved to be shaken not stirred. I am glad about our marriage. Why don't you tell me a story".

"That's what I have been doing all these years"

"No. I want a bed time story in full. Since it is only 7 P.M., you can complete the story".

"I cannot forget our first date. I thought I was going to be put on a leash".

"You deserved to be brought into civilization"

"I was brought up by my parents in a civilized way. I am not Tarzan".

Both of them retired from service as Chief Managers. Raju retired three months before Leela. Leela is working as dubbing artist and singer. She also directed music for a couple of movies. She teaches carnatic music. Raju was working as a coach for Karate and for physical fitness. His work was mostly in the morning. Leela also tries to be free in the evenings whenever possible. When they were posted at different places, Raju could not bear the separation, but it was inevitable. After retirement, Raju became more attached to Leela. He missed her if she was with the neighbours for fifteen minutes. Her absence, when it was inevitable, made him feel miserable. One day when Leela was at the studio recording a song, he was sitting gloomily and expressed his feelings to his daughter. She said, "Nanna, Amma has gone for only five minutes. You are hopeless"

Leela interrupted his thoughts and asked, "Are you going to tell the story or not"

"I will. Just give me a few minutes. I wonder how I put up with you for forty years"

Anticipating his story, his daughter and grand children and mother-in-law and music students sat around. Her parents did them enormous service. When Leela and Raju were transferred, their daughter was taken care of by them so that the child didn't have to change schools. Besides, Leela and Raju were working at different places.

Raju said, "I don't have a stock of bed time stories in my memory. I spin a yarn for the moment. Now listen to this fresh story created exclusively for you. Long long ago, but not very long ago, nobody knows how long ago, there lived a man"

Leela intercepted," That is from an old movie. Cut the fancy stuff out and go on with the story".

"O.K, about ten years ago, there lived a man of twenty five years of age in a village near the Nallamala forest near Srisailam. He was moderately educated and was working for a timber trader on the left side of Srisailam. He was not happy. He wanted to make it big. He did not know how to go about. He prepared a list of things he wants to lead a happy life.

He decided to seek divine intervention. He went into the forest, found a suitable place deep in the jungle, where nobody comes. He found a rock and sat on it like a maharishi and started meditation(Tapas). After one year, he stood up on one leg and continued the invocation of God. After six months, he changed his leg and continued for another six months. He later sat on his knees and repeated his mantra to invoke God for one year. He later stood upside down and meditated for almost a year.

He did not stir in rain, cold and Sun. He did not move from his place for food or bath etc. When he was upside down, the long beard that had grown over the years bent down and covered his face. One day a tiger came to the nearby bush following the scent of a human prey. It crouched and crawled towards him. It was surprised at the human who ignored him. It came close to him and smelled. The scent was so nauseating, the tiger vomited and ran away.

A few days later, the man heard a voice calling him by name. It took the person at least one hour to wake him up from the trance. He opened his eyes but could not see. The voice said, "If you part your beard, you can see me". He did so and had seen a divine personality with traditional silk Dhoti and his shoulder piece. He had a golden crown on his head. He was also postured upside down.

The man asked, 'Who are you?'

'I am from Indra's secretariat'

'How long have I been doing this meditation?'

'Nearly four years'

'You have come very early. The ancient Rishis were meditating for decades before someone from heaven showed up'.

'Those days were different. Large number of people were seeking divine help. The secretariat was short of staff. The Rishis were seeking things beyond the discretion of Indra'

'Why are you standing upside down?'

'I am trying to talk to you face to face. I cannot talk to your feet. Shall we return to normal posture. My head gear is slipping and may fall. Don't return to the normal posture immediately. First lie down. After some time, sit up and wait for half-an-hour, and then stand up slowly. I will wait." The man did as he was told. His beard was thick and hard. It was still covering his face. The messenger from heaven told him not to remove his hand, and hold the beard down.

The man said, 'I still think that you are very early.'

'True. We are trans-dimensional creatures. One year in our world is equal to several hundred years of the earth year. Nobody has been performing Tapas in this yuga. Your four years is equal to less than a second in our world. When the beep and light in the system indicated that somebody was on a hard Tapas, we thought that there was voltage fluctuation. The light was on and the beep was working normally. Even in the case of ancient Rishis, we were responding within a quarter of an hour in our world.'

'Why are you wearing a mask over your nose and mouth?'

'You stink. Nobody can stand that smell. I also have naphthalene balls in the mask. What do you want? You have performed well and deserve the boon/or boons according to your eligibility.'

'After four years of trance, I forgot why I did this?'

'I can ask you to tell me your mother's maiden surname, your father's place of birth etc., but you are not registered with us.'

'What shall we do now? I had a list of my requirements, but I do not remember any of them.'

'Do you have a grievance against anybody. I will help you settle things with him. This is in addition to your list of boons. I can do that with in my discretion and nobody needs to know about it.'

There was the sound of soft snoring. It was his mother-in-law. She had fallen asleep. The others are awake, but the children appear to be close to dozing.

"Shall I stop. I may disturb your mother."

"No, continue with the story. She has fallen into sound sleep. She needs to take sleeping pills every night. Your story has made her sleep naturally".

"The kids also are likely to go to sleep".

"I am surprised at your talent. You can tell stories which are so boring, you go to sleep telling them".

"That is not a compliment"

"It was not intended to be. From now on, you are going to tell my mother bed time stories every night"

"If I go to sleep half way, I may be sharing her bed".

"That is a valid point even though it is ridiculous. We will record your stories and give it to her. When she goes to sleep, I will switch it off"

"Continue with the story"

"Where was I?"

"The man was offered help to equalise an insult"

"Ah! I got it. The man said, 'The trader I worked with insulted me several times. I would like to repay him'.

'Fine. I do not like to miss this opportunity. We will go to him now. Get close to him and scream but keep at least two feet away from him. Any closer, he might die.'

'I do not get your point.'

'You stink so terribly, that you do not need a weapon to kill anybody. Get close to the enemy and scream. The stench will kill him.'

'I do not want to kill anybody.'

'That is why you should keep at least two feet away.'

The revenge was sweet and the strategy was fantastic.

Indra's messenger asked, 'you must tell me what you want. I cannot stay here forever.'

'I don't remember any of my wishes. Please do what is best for me. I want to lead a happy, luxurious life in this world and come to heaven after my death. I leave everything to you.'

'That means we have to keep a man watching you always. That will not be difficult. I will convey your request to the boss. He will oblige. That is within his discretion. Your request is reasonable. It is most likely that the man allotted to you may doze off. If you do not get help in dire situation, recite your mantra several times. You need not say it aloud. We hear the mind too. It is nice to meet you. Good Bye. Go back to your place and live happily. I will get you dressed up properly'.

So saying, the messenger disappeared. The man lost his beard, hair and all dirty stinking things and became a well dressed, handsome person.

And he lived happily ever after".

The children and daughter were sleeping soundly.

Leela said, "You certainly have a talent. It was a great effort for me to stay awake. All the others have gone to sleep at the odd hour of 7.15 P.M.

"Because it is only 7.30 PM now, I am awake. Normally, I would have gone to sleep when the man completed two years of meditation".

"From tomorrow, your duty from 3.30 PM to 5.30 PM is to record your stories. We will reserve the copyright and release CD in the market for people who are unable to go to sleep. If anybody survives the first story in full, that is an acute problem. We will record more boring stories for them".

"You are making me feel proud of my talent. I admire you and consider myself lucky to have you as my wife".